SECOND

SON

SECOND

A NOVEL BY
Robert Ferro

CROWN PUBLISHERS, INC./NEW YORK

SON

Published by Crown Publishers, Inc., 225 Park Avenue South, New York, New York 10003 and represented in Canada by the Canadian MANDA Group.

CROWN is a trademark of Crown Publishers, Inc.

Manufactured in the United States of America

Library of Congress Cataloging-in-Publication Data

Ferro, Robert.
  Second son.

  I. Title.
PS3556.E76S4 1988   813'.54   87-27260
ISBN 0-517-56815-2

Book design by June Marie Bennett

10 9 8 7 6 5 4 3 2 1

First Edition

For Michael Grumley

To the Memory of
Bill Whitehead

You are looking very well.
Weren't you clever, dear, to survive?

I've a sorry tale to tell.
I escaped more dead than alive.

Candide

PART

ONE

After some time he realized the house was speaking to whomever might be listening: this was Mark. He heard it in the wind through the porch, in the boom at the end when a door slammed, in the whine of the furnace when first engaged; sounds that held images the house reminded him not to forget, images of moments fractured in air as when, turning at the banister at the top of the stairs, he saw his young niece tilt her head to listen to her vanity and adjust a gypsy earring—a languorous, emblematic moment of her magic childhood, in an older safer world. The house made this possible. He could see it still in the air.

Images also, besides his family, of the two strangers who long ago had built the house and lived in it and died upstairs: the Birds. Captain Bird, it appeared. The childless Birds had never struck such chords, while the numerous Valerians, occupying every room, adding others, had changed the house into something alive and hovering, a huge pet that loved them, vitally interested in the goings-on. Captain Bird however had seen to it that everything about the place was nautically and astronomically sound. It faced exactly east, on a line drawn up the middle, like a keel, that passed through the center of the hearth and out the bay window into the heart of the sea with the sudden precision of the speed of light. The sea, visible from every room, was in some rooms a wall; in others a picture on the wall. From the upper windows it seemed you were on a riverboat, and in winter, with the furnace, as if the whole place was under way, moving through a delta; approximately. From the long deck over the porch, leaning into the wind, he could see the sharp edge of the planet he was on.

Mark was ill, dying perhaps. He stood at the window downstairs—the window toward the pond, as opposed to the one toward the ocean, or toward the lighthouse. Its view contained a wedge of sea on the right, high after a storm and figuratively rushing across a bight of beach as if to flood the house. A man with a metal detector was weaving an invisible herringbone pattern across the sand, feathering back and forth along the beach, now and then scooping up small amounts of sand with a long-armed basket. Within the ranging intimacy of his binoculars Mark could almost hear the electronic *ping* of the metal detector as the man suddenly stopped.

This small drama: the man drops to a crouch. After two or three diggings in the sand, the little metal scoop proves inadequate. Only the human hand will do. The man is young, distantly handsome. Through his binoculars Mark can see the cold, downlike glow on his cheek. Fingers touch something that then is held up. It glints. Again the young man takes up the scoop and detector, glances for an instant up at the house, perhaps sees Mark in the window, and resumes the inferred pattern along the beach.

Mark's heart is thumping. What had he seen? Someone searching for valuables on the beach. His beach. Taking a deep breath he calmed himself. His sister Vita, had she been present, would have an explanation. An obvious metaphor, she would say, considering his illness, but useful. Mark might feel that much of his life lay buried on the beach—to be found and pocketed indifferently. This could be it, he thought. Or was it that the man with the metal detector was handsome? Perhaps Mark, being alone and frightened, merely wanted company—to talk—but wanted it as a pale vestige, in all its dimmer configurations, of desire.

Like the Birds before her, Mark's mother had died upstairs, eclipsing those two earlier, less-felt deaths, and claiming the house at last and utterly from its builders. Their two transparent shades faded further and Mrs Valerian's presence took over, as had been her intention. Her dying one year before, from a series of hemorrhagic strokes, had overlapped in an ironic but intentional way with an extensive restoration of the house—two processes sharing themes and schedules along similar though reversed lines: an Egyptian way of death, in which a place for the abiding comfort of the spirit is prepared. Mrs Valerian had theorized that the house would bind its occupants—her family—to her after she was gone. She had concluded that she herself would also be bound, an intention to be evoked with her name and memory by whoever entered the house.

Restoration had required a lot of money, thousands every week for months. This was regarded as a medical expense by Mr Valerian, who on the surface appeared to be rich, and who on the surface was, and he willingly gave whatever was needed because doing so assuaged his helplessness and grief. You could do nothing about a stroke, but the roof could be changed, and even the roof-line. On the ocean side windows could be cut to improve the views and lighten the interiors, with the immediate effect of liberation, as if something trapped inside the house, the Birds themselves, were at last released. Ten rooms of curtains, a dozen new rugs, every stick of furniture restored—the house emptied into a huge van and hauled to a penitentiary in Pennsylvania for refinishing. This had been arranged by Mr Valerian, a person not averse to pursuing a bargain across state lines. Mark had asked if this meant their furniture would be stripped by convicts with guns held at their backs—the sort of question his father found surprising. Outside, the garden was reconsidered, with spaces around the house pushed back so that new sweeps of lawn were created where sea rose and masses of creeper and honeysuckle had stolen up over the years nearly to the porch. A different curve was cut for the drive, as if Margaret Valerian, in her imagination, had flown up above the house and looked down to select the ideal line. These improvements went on all at once with a number of different crews and loud machines. After the broad measures came the smaller, meaningful ones—with outside the new garden, a dozen trees, a fence—all corresponding to the different phases of Mrs Valerian's decline, in which every day some new deficiency appeared or matured. As she deteriorated she rested her ruined mind on the new stability of the house, its lovely air of completion and bounty. Each day she went in a wheelchair room to room to see everything in its place, fixed by rules of association and design. Beyond regular use of the wheelchair, she lay propped on pillows, regarding the sea through the big window in her room. On the best and dwindling days Mark read to her from a pile of cookbooks—recipes like short plotted stories, with twists, nuance, surprises and uncertain endings, success by no means assured. To these details she listened closely, as to a chronicle of mysterious events. And when finally she died, it was with everyone around her, after a long and decorous farewell commensurate with the many months of the other sort of preparation. Light played over her face. Mark kissed her cheek and felt her spirit swirl into an angle of the ceiling, like perfume seeping through the house, a faintness of scent relative to its distance from her room—all of it lingering behind as planned.

He could not then agree, precipitously, to a plan to sell the house. Odd that all her labors and intentions, her clearly expressed wishes, should now be used against her. For no one could bear the accomplishment: that she permeated the place. For months everyone but Mark avoided it. And the upkeep, coupled with an obvious enhancement of the site, made its sale an ongoing temptation that grew. Why keep it when no one but Mark cared to use it? Someone had approached Mr Valerian with a blank check, willing to pay anything, anything at all. Here would be life's financial truncation of the dilemma. To discuss the matter, and since Margaret had left the house in their names, Mr Valerian invited the children to his house in a Philadelphia suburb.

None of them had been there in a year. Not a thing, not a stick, had been changed since the onset of Margaret's illness three years before. In his grief Mr Valerian was reassured by the certainty of things as they were, like a blind person who has memorized the layout. In a state of only slightly diminished mourning, now ritualized, he relied on the illusion of permanence, of repetition and changelessness. The legs of chairs sat in invariable indentations in the thick rugs, so that if moved they could be put back exactly, with the precision of landmarks. They *were* landmarks. Everything in the house referred to something else—something absent.

The fact that it was their first gathering in this house since the funeral brought back all the same feelings, so that Mark at first sat in a daze in the huge den while Mr Valerian outlined the situation.

"This came in the mail," he said, holding up the check. "Some people have too much money, and rocks in their head." He handed the check to his older son George, who held it with both hands, a live delicate thing, and shook his head in wonder. George handed it over to Vita, sitting on the couch beside Mark. Together they examined it for clues to such extravagant behavior.

George said, "We could get as much as a million dollars . . ."

"It's worth much more than that," Mark dropped in. He knew something about real estate since he had chosen to spend his time landscaping gardens professionally; with some success, since there were so many gardens, and people with so much money they mailed out blank checks to buy whatever caught their eye. Mark thought he overvalued the beach house because of its associations and his outright love for it; but its location directly on the sea, surrounded by empty buildable lots, the last in the area, had made the place more valuable than even he imagined. His younger sister Tessa came over and took the check from Vita. "Oh my god." She covered her mouth.

"So let's write in two million," her husband Neil said.

"Two million dollars?" Tessa exclaimed. "Are you kidding?"

"Four lots at five hundred thousand each," Neil said calmly. "Forget the house. They could bulldoze it and put up condominiums."

Mr Valerian's eyes, and those of his son George, glittered. "Is it zoned for that?" George asked. And Mr Valerian said Find out.

"What is this?" Mark demanded. "Aren't you all rushing things? I want you to know I will never agree to sell. You know Mom never would have . . . That house is neutral ground, for all of us. We're supposed to be together there."

"Mark." George turned to his brother from between the wings of a tall chair, the mate to one Mr Valerian invariably occupied. "Two million dollars," he repeated slowly.

"I don't care. It's been . . . It's too soon. You just

can't do it. Besides, it's worth more and more each year
. . . If you're just thinking of the money . . ."

"I say sell it," his sister Vita declared suddenly, hers
for various reasons the pivotal vote. Mark turned to
her as if struck.

"But Vita . . ."

She gave him a look she sometimes felt it necessary
to give, a look of baleful seriousness that meant it was
time to absorb something difficult but real, and which
she felt would not go away on its own.

"But it can't be a question of money," he insisted.
"It's too important for that. The *house* is the legacy,
not the money . . . She wanted us to be there together,"
he repeated. "I know she did. You all know that." He
looked around the room at each of them. "How can
you think of letting it go?" he demanded. "If she were
here now she would slap your faces."

"Mark, come on . . ." Vita said.

"No. I won't agree. Ever." He got up and walked
out.

After Mrs Valerian's death, alone in the beach house,
Mark had moved into her room and slept in her bed.
This felt peculiar only on the first night. Margaret
Valerian's room, with its large bay window on the
ocean, was long and handsome, running the width of
the house, with fine views up and down the coast. It
was blue and white, with white taffeta curtains, Indian
rugs, and white lacquer furniture. Through the line of
windows the horizon stretched around like the true
walls of the room, making it immense, bringing in the
sea and sky with all its light. It was a room to wake up

in. At sunrise the lemon, red, and orange colors of the sun revolved over the white curtains like flame, drifting down the wall as the sun rose, as in a stateroom on an enormous, slowly listing ship. Outside the sea slapped the beach resolutely, but he would be awakened by the clamorous light. Next to the blue room was a green room, and then a pink, no longer pink but referred to as such after so many years. The green room had been Mark's. Now he slept in the blue.

He felt that nothing was more important to him than this house, and since no one else stood in this relation to it they would not have understood the degree to which, day by day, the obsession grew. He saw himself as its custodian and protector, its Mrs Danvers, the connection coming through the blue room, "... *the loveliest room in the house, the loveliest room you've ever seen.*" Like Mrs Danvers he was proud to show it to anyone who called—though callers were not automatically interested—alluding in a fond crazy gaze over objects and views to a special, mysterious, nostalgic association with the past, never specified. Mrs Warden, a neighbor passing by, had been brought into it on a bright sunny morning, when all the white and blue seemed edible, and had said excitedly that if this were her room she would never leave it. Exactly, Mark thought; a woman skilled in noisemaking. And in fact his mother had never left. Sometimes it seemed he might suddenly turn and catch a wispy glimpse.

But the others did not love the house in these terms; why should he so care? Its beauty, no doubt; its canopic aspects regarding his mother, and now, being ill, regarding him; the memory of thirty years there together.

This, while enough, overwhelmingly enough for Mark, was insufficient to them, for whom it remained a pretty house by the sea with associations. They might say to him and to all this emotion: why and so what? Were it not for Mark, things would be different—simply the profit really instead of the expense and upkeep. He had no firm answer for himself or them, for whom beauty and recollection, like danger, glamour, greed, hunger—everything but disappointment and desire—were concepts belonging to other people. In fact, he thought, they might not see themselves for what they were, since what Mark saw and what they saw were not the same—when they should have been. House and mother had belonged to all. All had been children here; he and Tessa practically the same age, Vita just three years older, only George very grown at fifteen.

They had peered in at the misted, dusty windows. To one side Mark saw the dead startled Birds withdraw backwards through a doorway. His father signaled disapproval by keeping his hands in his pockets. Furniture lay in the middle of the vast room stacked like expensive fuel before the bulky fieldstone fireplace. Mark stood and turned toward the sea, which tilted over him at a slant like a picture, the line of the horizon that day blurring higher into the sky than might seem normal—it was all so important. "Only on the ocean," Mrs Valerian had instructed the realtor. Downstairs the ancient furnace spread itself across the cellar like the roots of a banyan tree, funneling huge fat limbs along the ceiling and up through the house. Mr Valerian shook his head, Margaret shuddered. She wanted to see the bedrooms.

He was ten, Tessa nine, the first summer, living like the Birds. Mr Valerian was not yet so rich and they camped out at first. It was necessary to replace many of the windows right away. They were fake and did not open. Margaret Valerian repeated this unbelievingly. How could they be fake? The cost of thirty windows was thus added to the mortgage. The air then blew through it—as long ago Captain Bird, besides saving money, had feared the sea might some day enter at the portholes—and the long front room behind the porch became a deeper veranda in itself, open to the blue breeze. On the dune beside the house Mark built a network of sand channels down the incline, encouraging a pink rubber ball to travel from up there to down here as if under its own power, to fall with a snug plop into a pit at the end: the top, center, and bottom; the beginning, middle, and end; up coming down. As a metaphor it seemed to fit for a long time. Most things in life, including life itself, seemed to have articulated sections, discrete and separate and straightforward.

Some weeks after the meeting at Mr Valerian's, Vita came to the beach house. On a late fall morning, the same as a summer day but for a faded difference in the light, they sat with coffee on the enormous porch. Up and down, the beach lay empty for miles. Boats in the offing, gulls and the changing light, the broad planes of sea and sky—these bright pictures were framed by the porch supports. Vita spoke first. Given the weight of his feelings she had changed her mind: she would not now agree to sell the house. For this was the most important thing, that when a person felt strongly about an issue in life, it mustn't be ignored by others; for if it was, everything subsequent to it would turn out badly, even though there should seem to be no direct connection.

"Then why did you say you would sell?" he asked.

"Because I was tired of Pop's games," she replied. "He thinks we're beyond his control here." Mr Valerian, since being widowed, had not again set foot in the house. "I think," she said, "he believes that if it's sold we'll spend more time with him."

In the morning light, regarding the female version of his own face, Mark said, "Is it as simple as that?"

"In a way. But even without your objections they couldn't sell it now." *They* were the two Georges, father and brother. "Until other things are settled nothing will be done." Vita looked at him, took a sip of coffee. "Why is it so important to you?" she asked. "Have you thought?"

". . . Because of everything."

"Right. You mean, all the years . . ."

"And Mom. And . . ."

Vita squinted into the sun.

"There's something about this place, you know," he went on after a moment. "It's not just me. I think of the pure chance of it being ours. Only chance. You could never arrange something like this again in a thousand years."

"Mark, it's just a house."

"But look at it!"

"Yes, I know," she replied, glancing around her as in a crowd. "But it's still just a house."

"You could say that's just an ass you're sitting on, but you would hate to lose it."

"You mean, it's part of you."

"It seems so basic," he said. "So obvious . . . The house is ours. It's been ours for so long. It's beautiful. To me it represents everything, the past, the future."

"—Yes," Vita interrupted him, "I see that. But I was wondering if you could see the less obvious reasons . . ."

"Such as."

". . . Some sort of fear," she suggested.

He looked at her, startled. "Can't beauty be enough?"

"No," she replied. "Not usually."

Now when he entered a room or suddenly turned he encountered himself and his family, his siblings and nieces and parents, as if he had been mistaken in thinking them gone and himself alone. How could he be alone there again, except for a few moments at a time? It had become, besides, actually the sort of house that attracted people to it, in a daily ration of deliveries, the maid, plumber, carpenter, furnace man, the painter who never finished and seemed to work on his own; the alarm man, the gardeners. Mark would hear them on the gravel, or the too-loud bell would ring and he would see again the futility of thinking it was a house to be alone in. The others asked what he did with himself, knowing to themselves that he did, simply, everything and was endlessly busy. It was large, with every nook of it developed into something to be maintained. He would sit for a moment and realize the hatch at the top of the tower was ajar; when it was open the covers of magazines on the table by the fireplace, three floors below, lifted and settled on the coil of updraft swirling through the rooms. Or some quadrant of the lawn was being watered, or a storm the day before had misted the north-facing windows to a blur that must be squeegeed; or a drain at the back was loose, or moss had begun in the outdoor shower, as it did every year, a furry lime-green that called to mind the baroque grottoes of overachieved Italian villas. He was half inclined, scrubbing it away, to let it this year take hold.

With his mother gone, the house, far from ever being empty or complete or perfectly in order, was, beyond being a house, a place and monument. This is what the others did not see except in the passion with which he explained the undertaking of yet some new repair or project. For it was big enough never to be finished, and everything that was done to it—had been done to it— seemed to call up in him a progression of further things, as if it now itself kept a list for itself, a list far more ambitious than his own. When he tried to explain this to Vita she characteristically voiced her opinion: that he liked to think this was true, yet of necessity he would have to say it did not come from the house. "These are your standards and ideals," she said. "Within the process, *you* decide." She was no doubt right. Her field. But the *impulse* she described in him was met by something in the house as palpable as its present shape: the shape it would have in the future. When Mark looked at it in a particular way, he saw it suddenly as it eventually would look. He said to Vita, "It's not imagination. I imagine different features and improvements all the time. They don't occur. But sometimes I see something already done, all its details at once, and after that it's not a matter of imagination but of recollection of the actual thing."

Vita shook her head, willing though temporarily unable to follow. "You mean of course the imposition of your will . . ." she suggested. But he had meant that with the warp of experience folding back on itself, as did time, it was all on a great tape—racial memory, the Collective Unconscious her colleagues had been talking about for so long: history itself, the future; the larger flavorsome bits. The house had a soul, it had a history.

"But not a destiny," she interrupted. "It could be sold tomorrow, and then who would interpret these—visions? Who would have them?"

This was precisely the point, he pointed out. No one would. That was his department. Vita did not doubt the potency of the scheme, as it inspired him, as it affected them all. Four or five weeks each summer she basked in this perfection like Princess Grace in the Monaco of her dreams. The rest of the year, with her children and their commitments, with her job and career, it was as with the others a question of the odd weekend. They might have held on to the place because the original investment was so eternally dwarfed by modern value—this was the Monaco of everyone's dreams—or now because of Mark; but without him keeping track none of it would have worked. Mrs Valerian had managed it alone for thirty years. Now he did, in his own way. They all saw his reasons overlapped with their own in letting him.

Odd that four such people should turn up in the same family, or odd that he should be among them; for it was Mark who made the collection strange, who set the curve, with his inverted sexuality, sensitivities and thin skin, his standards and thoughts from some other, different place. While they seemed or were strange only in these comparisons with him, which threw them to the opposite ends of all these spectra—George Jr, practical and cunning; Vita, evolved and cool; Tessa the winning, excitable wife and mother, still young, steeped in the details of her children's lives—all so different from Mark and now abundantly clear, after years when it had seemed otherwise. The gallant struggle to convince themselves and the world that he was merely another sort of Valerian—rather like Mrs Valerian, whose instincts in all of this had been unwavering—this struggle in the end had been incorporated into the great Filial Wars, pitched battles between Mark and his father that had dragged on for a decade, and in which the heaviest losses had seemed as usual to be innocent civilians: the family itself. It seemed to him his mother had given her life as part of this prolonged struggle, the only evidence at first of how deadly such things became if not settled early and wisely through ambassadors. They, he now supposed, were the ambassadors. He felt that the exhausted truce lately reached between his father and himself represented the world's last opportunity to avoid catastrophe. It was, as Vita said, a question of not denying something vitally important to someone else. If you did, it more than harmed you; it destroyed you and your world to the extent it was itself destroyed. Now his mother was dead, his father already old, and he himself apparently dying, although you could never, he had learned, be sure who would die before whom.

Vita did not in the least cavil, or hesitate. Like many

of his conclusions this came out in conversation with her. She thought the force of Mark's will, being thwarted by this immovable object—his father—had been turned back on himself with devastating results, and that evidence of this effect would subsequently pull his father down.

"You must cure yourself," Vita said, going right to the payoff—these were not office hours with a stranger, he thought. Meaning that if he could turn the process off he might neutralize its effects in time, and so at least slow the disease, or convert or divert it elsewhere. This was the idea, to buy time.

The stupendous news of his illness had abruptly ended the Filial Wars, like a smothered blaze. In the driveway of the beach house, where Mr Valerian would come to discuss it and see for himself, they embraced and wept. It no longer meant a great deal that Mr Valerian could weep, although there had been an era—most of their lives—when the idea itself represented a kind of doom not to be envisioned; while Mark, in compensation, had been always a person to weep as easily and effortlessly as an actor. Together they wept in each other's arms in a way that might have obviated all unpleasantness, if only, if only; the unfortunate misapprehension of one person, meaning well but getting it wrong, by another; he and his father weeping beside the gleaming automobile that then, a moment later, slid across the white sweep of gravel and carried his father away.

In the huge unnaturalness of the world the most unnatural thing is the death of a child, which is to say death out of order. In Mr Valerian's mind his son's illness sat at the top of a pile of problems that appeared to constitute this last segment of his own life. It took stepping back, but from his point of view it seemed, as he would presently say to Mark, that if they could only change places all this nonsense would be resolved, beginning with the medical thing which, of everything, was most beyond his control.

The other great problem in his life concerned the collapse at the last moment of the greatest deal of his long and profitable business career—the sale of Marval Products itself, Mr Valerian's life work, to Court Industries. This collapse, coming only hours after he learned of his son's illness, had transpired with an equal force of devastation, like a second bomb dropped on rubble. In a long moment of realization Mr Valerian had thought the two events to be in some way connected (as subsequently did Mark) beyond the usual compounded coincidences of life; as if, had you thought in astrological terms, which Mr Valerian did not, you might find that on this day and at this hour several planetary masses had aligned themselves toward his specific ruination.

But that it should happen now, and so quickly, in this mad, last-minute upheaval of his life; that here at the top of the monument you found not a statue, not the figure of Victory poised for flight, but instead pigeon shit and disappointment—Mr Valerian's disgust at this was less effective as a demonstration against life than it had been over the years against his mortified children. He was a man who had always intimidated people. He looked at them and dealt with them until he saw a light of defiance go out in their eyes. He kept on until he saw it, minutes or years. At last, in the drive-way of the beach house, he saw it in Mark's eyes. Help me, they said: it was all Mr Valerian had ever wanted to hear.

With something extra in her voice, due to the fact she was discussing her own father clinically, but also for what she considered the endless resourcefulness of the subject, Vita described Mr Valerian as "very heav-ily defended." The fortress of their father's mind, Mark thought, thinking of something rocky and impregnable by Baldasare Peruzzi. "If such a structure collapses, it comes down all at once," she said. "At the end the mind is ruined. Much better if somehow it holds together."

Mark's opinion of his father in these later years had thus been based, he felt, on this other resident expert—for what was Vita but court psychologist? the best money could buy, and right there in the family, rather like the best legal advice from their brother George. Bolstered by the respect he felt for Vita's mind, Mark had applied these opinions to his own situation: the Filial Wars. It was from Vita he realized he would never convince his father of the legitimacy of his cause; quite simply because Mr Valerian saw homosexuality in religious terms—as a sin—which then threatened the great buttress of his own defense system: Religion. The top third of all widowers, Vita reported, meaning in health and adjustment, survived with the help of strong religious beliefs. Thus Mark's orientation ran in con-flict with his father's concept of survival. Not a ques-tion of live and let live, Mark saw with dismay. It meant he must think of his father's generation as entrenched and lost—as of course they all thought of his.

For he *was* different from them—from his own father and sisters, especially different from his brother. He had something of his mother in him but this was because he realized that in the end only her love was unconditional, and in gratitude he had emulated her. Only that much of this appropriation did not sit so gracefully on him, the strapping male, as it had on her. And perhaps he had chosen some of her more problematic traits—the tendency to catastrophe for instance, of immediately expecting the worst in an unpleasant situation, hardly important but negative, and which seldom turned out as badly as she expected. He heard a variant of this in himself and recognized it as surely as an old piece of clothing that fitted him but belonged to someone else: his mother's sense of catastrophe. This had stuck.

Ah, the victim. This, too, she had allowed, had encouraged in herself until too late. She had proved to him that the victim creates and perpetuates himself. This was the embarrassing part of being ill. The metaphor here was also too tellingly clear: the homosexual as victim. Unfair to pin it on his mother, who would be indignant to be thought of in these terms. But it was Vita's point that this was the cycle to be interrupted if he would break the pattern and save himself.

Yes, Vita, but how? And for a long time—most of his life, and often even now—he'd thought of this difference between himself and his family as evidence not of his failings, but theirs. Was not the absence of beauty the ugliest thing in life? (Vita would say no.) In the general scheme of things among the Valerians he often felt that wrong choices won out over right—wrong ideas, wrong directions, wrong fears. From an early age he had spoken up, feeling that in this small crowd was room—the dimensions—for more than one opinion; or even two. After all, a family might advance, as in certain quiz programs on TV in which a whole generation, sometimes two or three, put their heads together to define reality, and for their efforts won a car. It seemed the diversity he offered might be of use to them as a family, if they could only see it that way. In this his mother half the time had been his ally; half the time, with a gimlet eye, not. In matters of taste at least—of form, decoration, aesthetics: the usual homosexual métier—they had long since looked to him for quasi-professional guidance; so that George Jr was legal, Vita psychological, Mark . . . artistic—though it might be argued that this end of things lay otherwise vacant of opinion for cultural, sexist reasons.

—Different, too, in that he was alone. This was it. Each of them had a unit of his own, while Mark clung to an order that had outgrown itself, whose vestigial remains could be found only in his father and himself, and in a ghost of the enmity between them, now laid to rest by . . . by It. The occasions on which the five of them might collude had been reduced to those of state—the meeting about selling the house for instance—or perhaps when Tessa, whose instincts, though less developed, ran along similar lines, might suggest a public lunch on Father's Day—just them—which, however, George Jr would be too busy and overworked to attend. It was not that they thought any less of the idea than Mark; if anything they thought more. Simply that family meant their own brood and not the abstract enshrinement, as if in retrospect, of the Valerians as they one day might have been but were no more—something in Mark's imagination. He might make every effort to impose this vision on them—the fight for the beach house had been one such effort—of a caring, interlocked group of siblings. But the demands of their own children made this difficult, except at intervals, or when a flare of need went up over the life of one of them. It was not that it didn't exist, this idea of family, but that it did not seem to exist always, and never as Mark saw it; or if it did, which he saw it did, it was really only among each of them and for their very own.

Meaning that he was not a member, in each case, of *their very own*. Here we had musical families, like musical chairs—life was nothing but quiz programs and time-passing competitions—and when the music stopped he alone stood in the circle of upturned, satisfied faces. None could feel this sense of estrangement, apartness, because all of life's institutions had seen to it that they didn't. Mates, children, parents, and other siblings all fitted into arrangements laid out for this specific accomplishment: to belong. So much easier, he thought, for them to go along—unnatural not to—because for them it was stupefyingly enjoyable, one small triumph of legitimacy after another.

But did he really expect family life to be arranged around the requirements of spinster aunts and bachelor uncles? Freud would say Grow up. The burden of neurosis added to the weight of history was too great. Darwin would call Mark's kind a mad biological experiment teetering on the edge of extinction and doomed to failure. Both privately would shake their heads; though Freud, being Jewish, would wonder. Vita, their avatar and spokesperson, would say that, considering the twenty-six million Americans extrapolated from Kinsey to be gay—one in ten—some people slipped through history without ever reaping its rewards.

It did not do to complain, but to understand. Her analogy was in this case the primeval tree of primitive man. Mark knew it as a two-story tree house he had built at an early age with Donny and Brock. It popped so immediately into mind that he knew she was right.

"But can we not provide some other service? Is it all just the timely impregnation of females?" he asked indignantly.

"What else did you have in mind?" Vita replied dryly. ". . . You may of course sound the alarm. But life is not that simple. Sometimes sounding the alarm arouses passions and causes trouble. In the commotion branches break, people fall and hurt themselves. The leopard grabs one of them . . ."

"But without them . . ." Mark said weakly. He would never be convinced.

In these conversations Mark was aware of this same weight of respect coming across the line from his sister. What was it in him that held her interest? Creativity, he thought; the position engendered by a combination of male egotism—the inculcation of centuries—and a feminine passivity, rarely mixed in those days, openly; or at least in her Philadelphia suburb. Only later did he see she had realized her professional luck in finding, in her own family, a fine pure example of something they were alluding to at school: Freud's obsessional neurotic. She of course made no effort to inform him of this conclusion, and he went on thinking she saw in him, at least potentially, the artist he wished to be. In any event, it would be one or the other; this was perhaps a matter of opinion, and too soon to say. Art, he thought too, was nothing but obsessional and neurotic. And what might have alarmed the sibling of another shrink seemed, to Mark, to be evidence of some sort of artistic progress not otherwise obvious.

He was less different from Vita, perhaps because they had in their own way each been made to follow their brother George, with Mark's version matching hers in certain cross-gender ways; as if their parents, the Valerians, having thought just so far, had put everything into their first child and had made do, with the remnants of parentage, for the other three. George and Tessa were easier—not that *they* were similar—for being the first and the last. But Vita and Mark, appearing as if unbidden or at random, seemed to share the burden of catching their parents unawares, unprepared, or bereft, even though never in her marriage had Mrs Valerian made love without the thought of conceiving a child. How for instance did a little girl differ from a little boy? Why then was this second son, who had come from the same people and in the same way, so shockingly different? The Valerians, smug, oblivious and proud, did the best they knew how, making an awful mess, Vita thought; Mark thought. But then in those days who hadn't?

Mr Valerian stepped from the car and shaded his eyes from the sun. Perhaps he had been weeping on the drive down. Expecting him to the minute and hearing tires on the gravel, Mark came slowly out the door and through the garden, hands in his pockets, footprints blazing up behind him in tiny, sickle-shaped fires: his pockets spiritually picked, his life up in flames. Flowers in the border flashed dots of color at his feet, drifting by in focus within a long green blur. As he approached his father, they each wore the same ripening expression, of remorse and reproach, of colossal disappointment; this overlapping response paired their display—a sad caving-in of their feelings—and like two fine dynamos reaching tandem, they embraced. Mr Valerian pounded once, twice, on Mark's shoulder in an excess not of tenderness but anguish. He said into Mark's ear, "Believe me, if I could change places with you I'd do it in a second." It was what on the drive down he had decided to begin by saying. Holding his son by the shoulders, and at last seeing all defiance gone, he added, "We're going to go through this together, and there's nothing we can't do if we want." This sent them back into the vortex. Mark felt infantile, helpless. He was ill: something between the two of them had shifted into something manifest on its own, a third, evil thing set loose, against which both now were helpless. An alliance of his own resolve coupled with his father's was meant to bear some force against this, which, coming from within, must be pursued from within; though it appeared now, even in the abstract, beyond spiritual, intellectual, even emotional measures. Perhaps only the medical remained. Strength of intention his father meant to give him, not realism or facts but something to use in the coming fight, something abstract to fight something real, against which as yet no real weapons existed.

They came through the house into the sitting room. Being alone, Mark had ordered it with the precision and flair of a photo-stylist. The vast blue plane of sea stretched around. Mark could almost feel the little hop his father's heart took, of pride, recognition and pain at the purity of sudden association with Margaret. Mr Valerian looked out over the beach, nodded his head but sat in a chair with his back to the view—a gesture that meant here again were reasons why, with one thing and another, he was unable to enjoy this house further. They sat quietly. The waves squandered themselves. Two brown rabbits appeared on the lawn to feed, ears ruby sunlight. Mark watched them over his father's shoulder.

"Well," Mr Valerian began. "Tell me about this . . . Tell me what the doctors said, what—y'know—what you know about it." Put me in the picture, Mark thought his father had with a certain delicacy refrained from saying. The terminology of a business meeting seemed appropriate to the situation, certainly automatic. He saw that sometime in the next few minutes he himself would say, "The bottom line is that there's no cure."

"Look," his father exclaimed when this remark had been delivered, "that's where you're wrong. It's not the bottom line. You mustn't think that way. They'll find a cure. They're all looking . . ."

"Utter bullshit," Mark interrupted. "It's not a cure they're looking for, it's a vaccine. Protect the healthy, let the sick die off."

"But, Mark . . ." Mr Valerian protested, shaking his head.

"It's what they did with polio, and they were children."

"Well, you've got to think of yourself," his father went on. "You've got to be positive. You'll beat it one way or another. Either they'll find something or something will happen."

They regarded each other.

"And," his father said—these were the things he had driven here to explain—"I have a feeling this is a light case."

"A feeling?" Mark said.

"I just don't think it's as bad as you think."

"Dad, it's not what I think."

". . . And there's experimental things. I read yesterday there's a guy in California immune to everything. They're studying his blood . . ."

"I don't think this is something we'll be able to buy."

"Why the hell not?" Mr Valerian sat forward and went on in a fresh tone, "But you see, Mark, this is what I mean. You mustn't say, 'No, no, I can't, I can't, this is impossible, it won't work and I'm going to die . . .' You've got to think something will happen. Some goddamn clever Swede or Frog will find the answer . . . And you'll see. It's not as bad as you think—in your case."

"You only say that because you can't face it."

"Then what the hell are you going to do!" his father snapped, "—Lay down and die? Is that it?"

"I'm not going to kid myself because you want to hear it."

"And that's where you're wrong, my friend," Mr

Valerian said derisively. "Why not a miracle? Open yourself up to the idea that anything can happen, and you're going to get through this in one piece."

". . . Faith," Mark said quietly.

"Faith," Mr Valerian repeated, adding a slight though unmistakable measure of reverence.

Mr Valerian turned and they looked out the window together, each backing away from the idea just raised—Mark because he wished to avoid an argument about religion; Mr Valerian because, while relieved to have hit on something tangible, he was not prepared to pursue it. He knew prayer and hard work were the answer—had already begun his own program along these lines—but not until you came to it yourself. And Mark thought it time to say something about his father's other great problem: the collapse of the deal to sell Marval.

"George told me," he began—out to sea two little sailboats took different tacks on the same wind, sails pinned to the opposite reach, the one crossing the other's wake; Mark thought of the currents as invisible streets— ". . . about the rest of your day. I'm sorry this happened all at once."

"I don't want you to think twice about that," Mr Valerian replied. "It's a disappointment, that's all. It means more hard work when I would've been retiring. But I can deal with that sort of thing. I've been doing it all my life."

"All in the same day . . ." Mark said wonderingly.

"Yes, well . . ." His father turned away from the window.

They put together a lunch of odds and ends and ate

on the porch in front. Here Captain Bird had most seriously contrived to duplicate, on dry land and for the enjoyment of his dwindling days, the unique commanding experience of a ship's bridge. An end of the porch came around and finished in a circle topped with a pointed cone, like a gazebo jutting from a corner of the house. With the arrangement of a sand dune, a trellis, and the eastern orientation of the house, Captain Bird had created the illusion of being actually at sea, within a wheelhouse. If you sat or stood in a certain spot the horizon stretched three-quarters of the way around, the beach fell below the level of the porch railing, and all land disappeared, leaving only the sea. As they ate, a net of diamond shadows fell through the trellis, drifting over their shoulders and across the floor.

"What about George?" Mark said, to stay off It for a while. His father looked up. "What about him?"

"Well, he's disappointed, isn't he? He's worked hard on this, for a long time."

"Yes, he has." Mr Valerian had thought to learn something about George. Sometimes his children told each other things that then he heard secondhand, as intended. "He's got his practice to repair. This thing took a lot of his time."

In conversation, as otherwise, Margaret Valerian had been their connection, the buffer between them—in a way demonstrated by the damage she herself had sustained; by the worry, never clearly stated, that the wrong person being right, the right person wrong, and she herself never sure, not enough had been said or felt for either. Instead she had worked hard to make them comfortable, knowing mere comfort was never enough.

Mark and his father seemed only to disagree on principle, the principle of sex. This she held to be impossible, for love alone mattered, not principle. In fitting and tailoring their disparate responses to each other, she managed for years to fend off the implications and disasters of the Filial Wars, saying to one what the other could not. "Your father does not mean what he says. He loves you very much," and vice versa. So real was the need, any transparent effort worked. After her death the connection had devolved through necessities surrounding her funeral and burial—the plot, the monument—for if the beach house meant the survival of her memory and spirit in Mark's mind, even in her own, in Mr Valerian's a cemetery was where such things naturally came to rest. To him the beach house, besides being a sad reminder of his dead wife, or the dying one, was now his sole connection with Mark. And some months after Margaret's death, at the change of seasons—when fifty steps to wintering an old mansion on the water suddenly presented themselves—Mark had automatically taken up the job, interpreting this as an extension of his mother's wishes—and now, being ill, it seemed he might belong there as much as she—while Mr Valerian saw the opportunity as both practical and wise. Several years into the arrangement it had become and remained their subject. In every conversation, one or the other of them brought it up.

"How's the house?" his father said, sociable over the food.

"That depends," Mark replied, "on where you look."

Mr Valerian waved his hand in agreement. It was endlessly expensive, unfinished, yielding to salt air and sea. They were still compensating, thirty years later, for Captain Bird's economies. "That Bird," Mr Valerian would say, "had an anchor for brains." It had been some years before they discovered all the drains simply stopped below grade. All had to be dug up and connected. In his own mind Captain Bird had been constructing a boat. Nothing except her moorings must hold her. She must be free to sail at any moment, in the dead of night or day, straight to sea on the course so carefully drawn through the hearth. Now, Mark thought, the place was locked in—by water main, sewers, gas lines, TV cables, telephone wires, even the thin lightning rod of copper braid twisting from its height off the chimney and down the sides of the house like a package tied with cord.

In Mark's mind, as opposed to Captain Bird's, in the moment before setting sail, someone must sever these new connections one by one. Where possible over the years he himself had felt inclined to keep the boat idea in mind. An innovation of his own had been to shape the ocean-side lawn into a bow, with a white, chevron bulkhead pointing east into the waves. He thought that if this bow-shaped piece of earth were included, giving her deck space all around, it would be easier to fit the severed connections to a life-support system, all within a clear crystal cube containing the earth's atmosphere— on a fresh morning, the sun still on the water, or a starry night for sleeping, dreaming—a crystal ship of lights that silently slips her lines and sails away.

PART

TWO

Now you could say they were what they were, what they had intended, or what had been intended for them, if in general less so, and different in each case from each other, from what they each had been when young—always with the possible exception of George.

George Jr at forty-six was the *echt* lawyer, to whom a judge might say it was a pleasure to have him in court. He never lost a case and never to lose was never to imagine losing. George had gone beyond his father's dreams for a legal career, described to him in detail from the age of five by a man who with another chance at life, manifest in his son, had not hesitated to choose the Law. If you understand the law, Mr Valerian said, "and make it work for you . . ." by which he had meant not use of the law but of a lawyer you could absolutely trust: your own son. Both dicta had proved correct in Mr Valerian's life, and his greatest business successes had come after George Jr entered his legal prime. *Harvard Law Review*—a mountainous achievement in the family's so far rather flattish uplands—then clerkship to a state supreme court justice, followed by a career of steadfast yet inoffensive honesty; George's dreams for himself doubled back on all this into the dark-robed sanctity of universities, directorships, the Supreme Court itself. None of it was to be doubted. He had married a local girl, Claudia Kelly, although their story included the idea that they had at first, in high school, disliked each other. This might mean that even the most natural, the most automatic alliances required preparation and maturity. They had produced two girls, then years later at the last moment a boy and heir, although you didn't say this except with looks; a receptacle for all that otherwise would have flown about the house looking for rest: his dynastic dreams and thus hers, taken intact from his father and developed along modern lines. Having come so far, George Jr found himself really moved only by the idea of how far, proportionately, his own son might go. Having lived his life according to the happily concurrent wishes of Mr Valerian (it was something he had got in every word from his father's mouth) George felt no compunction in repeating the formula, rather in an identical way; and especially considering the quality of advice rendered in this case, where could his own son not reach? Mr Valerian himself now watched little George wistfully, nostalgically, knowingly. And as if stepping accidentally into the glow of this expectation, and as if George and Claudia knew that God rewarded such attitudes, the two little girls themselves excelled at any-thing they touched. Everyone had taken note of the success of this formula—traditional, strict but really untried, loving, supportive, a trifle meddlesome—by which they had produced three admirable, you would say special, individuals: Sarah, Abigail, and little George of course the Third. With George Jr's vast legal proceeds they had bought and, with Mark's help, restored and decorated a graceful old house in Philadelphia, in which a frank luxury dished the simpler houses of their youth.

Vita—whom Mark often called Life Itself, at which she would smile at being seen in the affectionately informal light otherwise discouraged by her doctorhood: "Dr Burke" struck the cool, almost severe, professional note she admired—Vita had chanced to live her life at the neap tide of Feminism, and to have been caught, in her late twenties, by some of its larger waves. Her insecurities, the ragtag insults and conundrums of modern chauvinism all were washed away, together with the attitudes and responses of the Chinese daughter better drowned; for the sudden obvious clarity of the world's ignorance relieved her of this burden. After nearly a decade of secondary ambitions, including carpentry, printing, even plumbing, by which she had sought to establish herself on the fringe of masculine achievement, and by which incidentally she proved herself the handiest of the handy, she threw it all over; and in a decisive shift of perspective saw a remedy for her own nearly desperate case: knowledge. Dispassionately, she would learn the secrets of her situation, and with an intelligent, detached program of intent would pull the fabled, but one could see already crumbling, structure down.

She went back to school. At thirty-eight, with a thesis on "Emotionalism in Early Suffragist Figures," she took a doctorate in psychology, using her estranged husband's name rather than her father's because quite consciously she wished to deprive him of the constant opportunity for remarks about a Doctor Valerian— another of his ambitions for the family, but one that had skipped her altogether, landing—a seed on dry ground—on the blood-fearing Mark. Henceforth Mark understood the cachet of titles, for his sister now became all she had never been; as if with this accomplishment she had transferred herself from one sort of existence and hemisphere into another; the one lacking, the other abundantly legitimate, even powerful: Dr Burke. Thereafter he sometimes also called her the good doctor, and realized that with this translation of herself from idea to substance, from a kind of female to a kind of male, she had made a success of her life; a realization she herself enjoyed, which had its own legitimizing effect. Having imposed a vision of herself on the world, the world went along. She was what she had seen herself as: a knowledgeable doctor—rather than what they had imagined her to be: a woman.

Before that she had borne four children, all girls. The Valerian gene pool was inclined to the distaff. These girls, who ranged at the onset of Mark's illness from fourteen to twenty-four, all bore the watermarks, some the scars, of their mother's turmoil and divorce, later mitigated by its mutually amiable outcome. The youngest and most troubled was afterwards lifted back to sunniness by the chatter and buoyancy of three unruffled sisters. Their father lived nearby with his second wife and fifth baby girl, a new group nonetheless included, welcome and natural, at holidays and principal Valerian rituals. Even by itself the connection would have held, but it was bolstered by Pat Burke's position as a vice president at Marval. He and Mr Valerian saw each other every workday of their lives.

In their float to the surface of suburban society each of Mark's siblings had decided on a stage among the Irish: Pat Burke, Claudia Kelly; Tessa's husband, Neil O'Hara. Mark felt Tessa might have chosen, instead of Neil, someone more like himself for a mate—an artist, an aesthete. But like Vita, she had brought home another businessman, as if precognitively and with Mr Valerian's eventual wishes in mind; for who could predict these things? Neil O'Hara had come a great distance to become a Valerian, as far nearly as Mr Valerian himself, of whom it could be said that both his daughters, in husbands, had done very well by him. He had got the two men early, or they him; and twenty years later they were indispensable to Marval, precisely in the way that Mark was not. From Mr Valerian's point of view here was a typical and telling example of the way life furnished you not with your dreams but their inexact approximations. In Mr Valerian's opinion, loyalty and ambition, without blood, did not run truly parallel, and in the end never converged. Thus, sons-in-law were not sons. Mr Valerian's master plan for himself, that is for his life, had been devised at an early age and revised and revised. It had called for five children—two girls and three boys—although four boys and a girl would have been personally as much to his taste. Girls were for ballast and collateral, and would marry well. The three boys would be employed as lawyer, businessman, and doctor. Mr Valerian himself would know which should be which. If he had sat about in reverie, this is what he dreamed.

But of course no. The fifth child had been miscarried, taking with it, him, her, the remnants of Margaret Valerian's reproductive talents and the businessman: the missing other. Furthermore, some absence in the resulting design—or perhaps something as simple as the overweening symmetry of two boys and two girls—had disallowed most permutations, fostering instead an endless dividing and separating, competing and comparing, not within Mr Valerian's mind but in theirs. They were not four children but two pairs, of which inevitably half were somehow disappointed, discouraged; and half overstimulated, overpraised. As a child George had been beastly to Vita, in what might then have been considered a predictable, even a normal way. "Only a girl would bruise so easily," he remarked, as if this lingering proof of his casual brutality—the marks on her arms—were an effort to make him look bad. Sometimes now you still heard this other attitude in him, an element of playful dominion, of treacherous humor, the glee of the cruel baby-sitter; all of which still induced sudden anger in Vita, whom no one else could ruffle even with catastrophe, especially with catastrophe. George alone could make her skittish, with a phrase, a tone of voice. This power George was always conscious of, as something perhaps Vita herself gave him, unnecessarily, from habit. But in return, as if in revenge, she exacted a response in him as sudden and infuriating as her own: the feeling that everything he had achieved was illusory and relatively worthless—the result of dogged ambition, of cynical reliance on an existing order that favored him above others; of obliviousness to all ideas that didn't further his own case. Even his effectiveness as a lawyer she threw back at him as evidence of stubbornness and cold egomania, together with a desire for money, comfort, status, and privilege.

And did Vita herself not desire these things? Yes, but the point was, she thought, that desire in her case was not enough; and this lack was now measured in her continued resentment and anger. It had been unfairly set up. In his own defense George would say with a change of tone, *the* tone, that Vita had done very well for herself, for which he was proud. And she, who otherwise delighted in the declension of motives, the explanation and derivation of intent, would look at him in sudden exasperation and say, "Oh, you're so full of shit." They had that dangerous sort of relationship: one of a kind, in that no one in either of their lives—in which otherwise each was regarded with egregious professional respect—spoke to them this way; certainly not clients, judge or juries, not his wife; nor anyone in Vita's life, including George himself, whose weapons instead were a kind of posturing, a Mussolini impression within a scenario in which always, just before the curtain, he triumphed. These scenes started innocuously, often going wrong through George's own tendency to want to sum up conversationally, in pronouncements that Vita saw invariably from a different angle. The idea that no one else in his life questioned this supercilious superiority made her hunt out every trace of it. The idea that he alone, from her old life, should be also the repository and stimulant of her most humiliating memories as a feminist, was galling. Ten or fifteen years into this new regime, the brat in him was exhausted, coming out only when he was angry at something else, and never for the sheer boyish joy of it. And after innumerable punitive raids, Vita saw that George's sharper chauvinistic points had been worn to nubs. Having learned the obvious catchwords and pitfalls, he avoided them. Sometimes his genuine surprise at offending her was evident; often not. But he would not knowingly hurt anyone, for he saw the connection between this and being hurt oneself. He owed his success as a lawyer to a pragmatic instinct of finding a way through. His was a talent for seeing around corners, around the corners of corners, wading into the unpredictable—Vita would say wallowing, like an alligator—loving the preparation involved. This was his problem with Vita. Their confrontations embarrassed him. He felt guilty, surprised, in the wrong; as if here the subject was The Modern Social Male and he was unprepared, having somehow neglected the requisite course work.

To say that Vita, on the other hand, had spent her adult life trying to professionalize herself, was another way of saying she had done everything possible to stamp out the little girl in her, for this she saw as her main point of vulnerability. Vita held that others' perceptions of oneself were a matter of projection, and in her brother's vestigial condescensions she saw the shadow of an image she had otherwise eradicated. Any slippage was maddening because it represented the continuing obstacles of her life and reminded her of early humiliations. George would always think he was superior, made more money, lived better, commanded a natural respect, not only for what he had done but for what he was; while deep down, because of the old weakness, the old order, part of Vita was inclined to agree with him, while another part resented them both.

Let it go. Both tried—this was where family came in: these were the things they loved each other in spite of, for it meant that harsh as they were, these ideas were binding. She would not get over the irritation until she had extracted the fatal detail between them and dealt with it. And how, considering the underlying and unreliable protectiveness of the *guilty* baby-sitter, could George stop himself from playing and replaying the same scene. In this way they were each other's goad toward being what they each thought they were. After many years, and as with the others, they were defined by who they were with each other, as compared to who they were with the rest of the world. And to a great degree, who each of them was in the outside world depended on these five relationships and their permutations.

The other pair had not got this idea of a burning issue between them. Tessa loved Mark as we love people without knowing them, or before we know them well, which is the family way: because fate and circumstance have willed it. They were fifteen months apart;

he had never wanted or taken anything of hers, nor she anything of his. From the small promontory of fifteen moons he had looked out for her. He had received her like a doll at the age of dolls; for years they had been each other's doll, he eventually one of many—the favored, live, growing doll who ranked at one time just below Louise the Invisible. Tessa had lived for dolls the way she now lived for motherhood; and to the degree that Mark would consent to and enjoy the duties of a large doll, they remained popular with each other. Now he had survived them all: the little wooden, porcelain, or cloth avatars of her living children, each with fragments of personality. Over the years they had numbered in the hundreds—workaday playmate dolls that wore out and were replaced; gorgeous dress-up show dolls, among which, and you knew them immediately by their long ruffles and lace, were a dozen or so individuals who had stood in her room in herbaceous array, skirts flared, under little puffs of veils, with glossy hair and crystalline eyes gazing into the half-distance of another dimension.

What she had wanted in her dolls she expected from life—beauty and consideration, decent companionship, a good coat, a little fun. Mark had been inclined as a child to sit about, not so much thinking as wondering what to do next, and had liked Tessa's endless absorption with the moment, revealed in constant suggestions for games, all of them domestic. The hiatus when each of them discovered playmates of their own sexes had made Mark, at least, realize that all their games lately had been in some way lacking and compensatory. But wide-eyed and mutely fascinated by the war between their older brother and sister, it had never occurred to them to behave this way with each other; and an underlying mutual gratitude swept them along, even now, without their quite knowing why. Once he had teased her, just the once. He found her sitting on a neighbor's steps, alone, crying miserably. What was the matter? he asked. Why was she crying? Because he wouldn't stop teasing her. Who? Mark asked, instantly prepared to do battle for her. She looked up at him, eyes filled with tears, cheeks red, dirty and adorable. "You!" she shouted accusingly, overcome by betrayal. It was the first time he realized one's acts had consequence. People were not dolls. He had been being a brat, a tease, a boy, like George. Perhaps Mark had not gone on with it because Tessa reacted with tears and pleading, instead of Vita's stoic defiance, who after all had been through it a thousand times. With Mark and Tessa it had never happened again.

Tessa could not be simply defined, even in part—like George, by his superb professionalism; or Vita, by her lift from inadequacy into something like personal power; or Mark, by his existence within the hyperbole of an artistic temperament. Tessa herself had each of these things—the professionalism, force of character, the hyperbole—but she had them without their objects: a profession, a firm idea of herself, or art. Perhaps she was as an emulsion of all of them. Mark didn't know. She didn't know. She seemed after her mother's death to be more like Mrs Valerian, as by an effort as conscious as the revival and preparation of Mrs Valerian's favorite recipes, or the use of a favored nail color; measures matched by others too subtle or obscure to recognize. Perhaps the strongest instinct enhanced in her was that of motherhood itself, and only a year after Margaret's death Tessa had given birth to a late third child, hardly anticipated but made welcome nonetheless, yet another little girl; and the devolving questions of Tessa's life, reemerging as her original two children had grown, fell back again, receding before the flooding instincts, the revived priorities of motherhood.

Tessa had felt at a loss for *something to do*. It had been her children, she always said. And now this last child meant more for coming after her own mother's death. Into this devotional object she would both pour and find a superb professionalism—motherhood; a power—over life and death; the power also of the art of exaggerating emotions, the hyperbole of being alive. And when someone said they thought it ironic that Margaret Valerian, a famous grandmother, knew nothing of this subsequent, tenth, final grandchild, Tessa smiled her ironic smile and said, "She knows." Because they knew, she and Mark. Together they built a nursery that involved the addition of an entire second floor to Tessa's otherwise modest house, thereby doubling its size, with the baby arriving the day after the curtains went up. If Mrs Valerian had left the world from the linerlike luxury of a Cape May beach house, little Margaret came down into a delicate confection of nursery allusions, not one lacking, and all executed in tiny Laura Ashley-ese: sprigs, rosebuds, two different patterns and a stripe, the deep protective rug, little lamps— the miniature boudoir of a miniature princess, ready just in time.

☆

Their father, George Valerian, was the wild card. His life had brought him from New York to Philadelphia as from one planet to another. His own siblings—who all lived in New York City—hardly knew him for what he had become, a kind of magnate, rich and apart. To these sisters and brothers George Valerian represented all that seldom occurs in life, or that occurs only to other people. Here, in him, and their view of him was greatly exaggerated, they were themselves lightly touched by success. Dreams of extrication from want, of the glamour of finery and excess, of fearlessness in restaurants and flights to sunny beaches, they associated with him. They envied him, seeing him as richer and happier than he was. And he in turn remembered them as what he had left behind, witnesses and proof of what he thought he had done and become.

None of it had ever changed, as none of it ever does. The weather of their lives swirled around them randomly; and it seemed that if you could go from the beginning to the end you would find innumerable distractions and surprises along the way but ultimately nothing in any of them that had not been there from the start, fixed and waiting. George Valerian had gone as far as altering the name by which the world knew him: Giorgio Valeriani. And even that had not mattered. Mark, named for his maternal grandfather, thought the name euphonious; he felt that Marco Valeriani showed through like pentimento, which it did. It meant the world took them for one thing while they were quite another—not wasplike and cool, but beelike and quick to anger and perhaps unpleasantness. When he lost his temper or fell flights into depression he thought, This is my blood which can't be changed.

After a lifetime of promise and hard work Mr Valerian had got to the point so often envisioned for himself, the moment at which he might go from being comfortable to being rich. But something about to happen usually dissolves. His company, Marval Products, had been named for Margaret Valerian of course, since the main metaphor in business at the time had been matrimonial, and the good auspices of a well-placed female had been considered indispensable; tokenism to obscure their exclusion from a world of men. Women seldom brought in big accounts, even in cosmetics, but never in Marval's field, which was mining equipment: small tools, drills, bits and augurs. Any interest in the search for base metals automatically put you in Marval's path, and everyone in the region used their drills. The company was thirty years old and Mr Valerian, now getting on, had been for some time eager to retire. A new generation had appeared on the other side of the table and at the other end of the phone; his old competitors were either dead or out of business. In a shift from a postwar to a prewar attitude, the metaphor for this new generation was not marriage and cooperation, but the hunt. The language they spoke, while familiar, was essentially different; in the old days it had been the custom first to rant and rave, like gorillas, to give warning. But this crowd, with a cool silent smile, sliced off your testicles. Traveling fast and light, a younger man might have done well in a game in which ruthless-

ness and deviousness were cultivated, but as a septua-
genarian Mr Valerian felt hampered by all he feared to
lose. His was the sort of wealth that suddenly changes
hands, like a finicky cat leaping to the floor: too much
oil stock held too long, two large houses, a fishing
yacht, the company itself.

Coming to Philadelphia from New Jersey to get away
from New York, the five Court brothers had approached
Marval originally with a request to manufacture the
prototype of a new drill, with the promise of contracts
on all future orders. The drill, universal within a certain range, had been by some unexpected chemical
process altered accidentally in the cooling, into a spoon-
shape that cut through the ground like cheese. New
alloys made it even harder than regular carbon-tip drills
of that range, the first such advance in twenty-five
years, and theoretically it was possible eventually to
reproduce it in every size.

The new drill swept the industry; within a few years
Court Industries had made millions on the New York
Exchange, while Marval remained merely comfortable.
Their relationship, however, had ripened at last into an
agreement of acquisition, to offset the Court brothers'
so far paperish reputation on the Exchange, and the
long process was begun of drawing up an agreement
that both sides could sign. Mr Valerian's money, stock
and options, conditions, timetables, new positions for
George Jr, Neil O'Hara, and Pat Burke: all this was
worked out. George had found ways for his father's
enormous profits to be protected from a ravening set of
taxes. George Jr himself would have eight percent of
the new company and sit on its board of directors, on

nearly an equal footing with a few of the Court brothers. Neil and Pat would remain as president and vice president of the new subsidiary. Mr Valerian would retain a vestigial connection as consultant—an office no one intended to utilize—together with the stock, and continued rent from the Marval buildings for five additional years; plus a sum of money not generally bandied, but fixed at something over three million dollars, to be counted out on the bed in cash, like a drug deal.

In business the collapse of a complex deal often occurs for reasons more subtle than those that might otherwise have meant success; and as usual, here, they were a matter of opinion and point of view. But all of this meant little beside the larger issue: that this sudden failure of the deal crippled Marval. Only under the protection of a powerful ally had recent capitalization and expansion made sense. Even the two computer systems had been linked to coordinate orders and inventories. When the security of these steady orders evaporated, Mr Valerian found himself in a dangerous position. His cash flow was gone, and his vendors—people from whom he regularly bought supplies—were sixty-day amnesiacs, in that if accounts were not settled every two months they forgot who you were.

In a series of quarterly increments in the following year he had borrowed heavily from the bank, who admitted they had gone willingly to the barn with Mr Valerian several times over the years, and who now, with confidence, eyed his other holdings—a small but choice collection of English furniture put together by Mark and a friend in the sixties; the boat, stock, beach house. Mr Valerian had already put up most of it, with his own house in Philadelphia mortgaged twice over. The beach house in Cape May had been spared only because, being listed under the names of his children, he could not mortgage or sell it without their permission. Because of this, and because even the bank loans were no longer enough, he had also sold, too soon he now saw, the large block of Court stock offered him in rude severance, and in which, understandably but wrongly, Mr Valerian had put too little faith. In the short time since he had let it go, the stock had risen thirteen points, making the Courts even richer, and costing Mr Valerian a substantial profit. It had all gone wrong.

It was thus perhaps, or should have been, easier to understand why Mr Valerian, at least, made no effort to follow the daily, even weekly course of Mark's illness—headaches, horrifying but painless new lesions, stress, panic, loneliness; the doom he read and heard about each day in the newspapers, TV, in people's eyes, since everyone must die. Mr Valerian had said he would try, that they would do this together, but the degree to which apparently they were all appalled and fearful seemed barely matched by a reservoir of family feeling: enough to allow for phone calls of commiseration and support—some successful, some not—but not enough to seek him out in Cape May, or to invite him to dinner in Philadelphia. It seemed easiest for Tessa, who called every week; and even Vita admitted she felt it difficult to respond. It was not easy to know how. Only a few days after one of them called, he would begin to add up the silences.

They seemed to think the tragedy lay in the fact that

one of them—so like Margaret—was leaving and therefore disrupting the family. This meant they would not now all grow old together. It did not appear they thought it anything less than logical that it should be Mark. And by extension of this idea he learned the implications of the illness. It was not just that he was sick; but that the disease, besides being tasteless, offensive on other than medical grounds, was considered dangerous in certain ways and was therefore feared and misunderstood, even by those who loved him. And so, besides his father and siblings, he told just three people, thereby joining yet another underclass: the secretly ill. Because he was looking for them, because he was where they might be—at the hospital where he went for appointments, in the streets outside—he saw and noticed these people, not ill until you looked closely, until you saw a telltale mark or lump or color, or lack of color; or noticed the sad, tired eyes, which all sick people had and which, beyond a certain point, could not be smiled away. He wondered if, should he be cured suddenly, this look would leave him: all pleasure gone, nothing about to happen. These few friends he told were sworn to secrecy; not to have included them might leave him with no one. Feeling cut off, he thought, was the same as cutting everyone off. He had seen Margaret turn her back and withdraw into herself and her inability to speak, to explain, as into the long view from her window. There it was: you saw it or you didn't. Her inability to speak, caused by the strokes, resembled now in Mark the inability to say why this had happened. Why was he ill? For the others, for the friends he told, an initial, shocking declaration had sufficed. Only for him was constant explanation required, the same unanswerable questions over and over: why and how? Beyond periodic exhortations to rouse himself from depression (because depression made him sicker) no one could think how to advise him. His several new doctors suggested that nothing be done for as long as possible, since any aggressive measures against the disease, far from helping anyone, had only killed them off: while among the untreated were those who had survived the longest. It was his idea to have the first lesions removed, little plugs of cookie flesh from three limbs; the fourth, his left leg, spared for no apparent reason. He slept a lot, taking long afternoon naps that divided the day in two; as if, in the remote removed darkness of his apartment in Philadelphia, or within the immediate brightness of the beach house, his days were shortened or doubled, while the nights were lengthened into long stretches that sleep could not completely cover. Occasionally panic arrived with fatigue, like an exhausted old man leading a sobbing child hysterical with fear. Nothing in his mind was changed or improved by sleep, but was neatened like a messy room.

All over the country doctors had arranged themselves in protective circles, like wagons awaiting attack, in research groups that pooled insufficient money and disciplines. Mark's own doctor belonged to a group in Philadelphia that had been formed early in the epidemic. Starting right after diagnosis, Mark had twice given blood for testing in vitro; now they wanted more, plus specimens of urine and semen.

Early in the morning, in a taxi crossing town, he wondered what it was in him that would enable him to produce semen under these circumstances. He had not had sex in nearly two years, had seldom masturbated. Such desire as occurred lasted only moments, as a fleeting response to sudden dazzling displays of beauty in the street. He wanted only to be well; and not being well preempted deep desire, even the wish for something more. Now, as the cab stopped at a red light, a tall black man crossed the street. He and Mark exchanged a look charged with sexual curiosity—big brown eyes, round and calm in a smooth face, locked with his, then softened in the start of a smile. At the other curb he smiled again and walked on. In Mark's virginal state, his own reaction constituted a kind of orgy of sexual feeling. In the old days he would have stopped the cab and leapt out to follow and meet the man. Instead he sat back complacently as the light changed and they drove away.

In the doctor's office he was met by an embarrassed Oriental who spoke little English and who knew none of the words necessary to explain what was expected on this occasion; though Mark understood that specimens would be taken before meeting the doctor. The Oriental handed him a small glass bottle and a plastic cup.

"You go here?" he suggested tentatively, indicating a lavatory off the corridor. He blushed and smiled in great pain.

"In here?" Mark asked. He turned, mortified, and went instead into the doctor's empty office where, understanding he was trapped and perhaps doomed, he stopped and burst into tears. The assistant put his hand on Mark's shoulder. "No, no . . . No cry! Doctor see you now," by which was meant perhaps that the doctor would not see him should there be tears. Mark could only think, as he took the bottle and cup, that here was the end of a line that had led from the center of countless dance floors, under dazzling lights, energy, protection, the insulation of endless youth, to this: a sterile, hopeless bathroom for the sick. He went in and locked the door.

He strove now to make some connection between a hospital and sex, something to help arouse himself; not simply from indifference and lassitude but from depression and impotence. He had thought, idly, they might perhaps have made available for this purpose a collection of skin magazines, some stimulus or other. But here was nothing but white tile. He removed his clothes, and urinated into the bottle, feeling the warmth of his body accumulate through the glass. He wondered at the color, the froth, and set it aside. He sat naked on the toilet.

Here was nothing. No substance, fullness, heat; the mind empty, the flesh soft, waiting to be put on. Again he wept since it all meant so much, more than tears could encompass. At his age, not old; with his advantages, which had been considerable; looking as he did, which was not bad after two years of illness and depression; it all led to this inability to get hard, for no reason other than the notion that his semen, so useless otherwise, was required for medical research. Not for love, beauty of man, or woman, not even for love of self (which might have been something) but for salvation.

But the tears had a peculiar effect, since after being sad they made him angry, and this at least was a real emotion. Some instinct developed in his vanished career in the art of love told him that behind anger lurked desire. He squeezed himself and clenched his innards, putting himself in mind of one image and another, until suddenly he thought of the black man in the street who had crossed in front of the taxicab—dark eyes, long stride, the beginning smile. This image walked into his mind as the man himself had walked in front of the cab, looking now at Mark with the same tenderness and availability. Here, here, Mark thought, feeling himself stir slightly in his hand. Raw sadness transposed itself. The connection was made. He did what one does, and with the plastic cup in one hand and his cock in the other, spilled out what was left of desire.

He dressed and left the lavatory, gave the two containers to the assistant who smiled his fierce smile—perhaps, Mark thought, in oriental admiration for the dramatic swings of the human spirit. He was shown back into the vacant office and invited to sit and wait. Afterward he learned that nobody liked this doctor; nor apparently did this matter to the man himself, for the unloved are always jaded, and this one found everything disappointing, lacking. But specifically Mark noticed he did not shake hands (as a sign of interest and medical fearlessness) or even look at Mark directly as he came into the office and sat down. He slid a paper across the desk and asked for a signature.

". . . permission to proceed with the program," he said.

"I would rather not sign until I know what the program is. Nobody . . ."

"—Nobody will do anything to anyone until we test your blood and semen," the doctor interrupted aggressively.

Mark took the paper and signed it. They regarded each other.

"What did your doctor tell you?" He was not one for names.

"Only that you are testing two drugs with a placebo, so there's a thirty-three percent chance of going untreated."

"That could save your life," the doctor said.

Mark asked what he meant.

"I mean that either of these drugs could kill you. This is not a game."

"A game? Did I imply I thought this was a game?"

"No, perhaps not . . ."

"You know, I'm sick," Mark said.

"Yes, of course."

"If there were somewhere else to go . . ."

The doctor pursed his lips, said nothing.

"You don't make this any easier," Mark said finally.

"I have fourteen people waiting with appointments."

"Didn't I have an appointment? Didn't I just jerk off in a jar?"

"Yes, and there's really nothing else to say about it until your specimens are tested."

"Then why not take thirty seconds to say that without the attitude?"

"Now just a minute . . ."

"If I don't have the right to a few minutes and a few questions, let's forget the whole thing."

"As you wish," the doctor said evenly.

Mark stood up. The paper he had signed lay on the bare desk between them.

"And the specimens?" the doctor asked.

"Drink them," Mark said quietly.

"Get out of my office. I don't have time for this." The doctor stood behind his desk.

Dr Thompson, his own doctor, confirmed this man's loathsome demeanor. The clash of a cold medical personality—detached, skeptical—with the fearfulness of victims aggravated by illness, was inevitable. Meanwhile Mark wondered if this incident had spared him dangerous risk; or had cost him his chance for a cure. How quick and tiny were the pivots of behavior. Some weeks later he heard that one of the drugs in question had been abandoned as ineffective, unavailing, toxic; and felt protected—though clearly this was an illusion— by a belief in his own instincts. Dr Thompson felt that Mark's untouched medical state constituted a kind of dowry, not to be squandered. It was all that was left of youth and a strong body. Mark needed their research and discoveries, but must be wary of which of them he chose, for afterwards he could not reclaim virginity and choose again. And they wanted and needed him because, more than a year after diagnosis, he was still comparatively unaffected. The disease was slow. Dr Thompson called it indolent.

At other times Dr Thompson said, "No answers, no answers," whenever Mark asked a question about research or theory, yes or no. During their appointments every two months, and then every month, they looked for new lumps and further lesions—the main reason for the visits—and it was clear after a while that with no answers there could in fact be no questions. Instead they talked about the way he felt, continued to feel. A radiation specialist, consulted about the problem on the bottom of his foot, said that really they could not do for him what he appeared to be doing for himself. This was vague but hopeful, although it meant also, unquestionably, that he was on his own.

Matthew Black was one of the people he told, an old friend from school who lived with his invalid mother in the lake country of Florida. Mrs Black could speak but not move, and lived in a nursing home in Gainesville; twice a week, Tuesdays and Saturdays, Matthew brought her home for the night and following day. In this way she did not feel institutionalized, Matthew did not feel guilty or overstrained. The rest of the time he was alone in the house on the lake. Every three or four months his married sister came from Nashville to give him a two-week break that usually he spent in New York City; sometimes he flew briefly to a European capital. Once a week he and Mark exchanged letters; this they had done for twenty years.

Matthew was a writer, to whom letters were important. He belonged to the last generation to value letter writing, the last children before television, in whom had survived a taste for less direct communication. Moreover, Matthew and Mark's relationship at school had begun on an intellectual footing and letters seemed a natural way to continue. For Mark they constituted a kind of journal. He had always told Matthew everything and occasionally this made his letters sound confessional; while Matthew distrusted personal revelation (domestic life with mother) as indiscreet, since it also involved her, and only occasionally let bits fall in an incomplete mosaic that Mark avidly assembled. They wrote to each other because it gave immediacy to what they did, had done; though their lives were different and, in Matthew's case, in no way immediate. He was reclusive, eccentric; at forty deep into middle age. Mark traveled, lived often in a different place in each successive season of the year, kept an apartment in Philadelphia, spent weeks at a time in Cape May, alone; could always find a flat to borrow or rent a few months in Rome, a habit since college. Mark had found, and continued to think, that moving from place to place stimulated and comforted him in ways another human being might have but hadn't.

Cape May April 1

Matthew,

It's that moment. Mummy is gone. The empty house is the same whether she has left for the day, or forever. A feeling of place and holiness. Time blows through it like a breeze, toward the past, with everyone; toward the future in which it is just you.

Do you follow? You have the advantage of having been to Cape May, while I have no idea what to picture for the Florida lakes—piles of pink nitrates alternating with small bodies of stagnant green water—which none but you has ever seen. I see a low ranch-style house on a biggish lake, shady inside and filled with colonial things like elephant-foot stools, turkey carpets and good silver, and not at all like those tall houses in Sayville. That is to say a house that guards against the sunlight and therefore embraces, encloses, enfolds the shady quiet; with a big clock in the hall, a distant motorboat on the lake. But you have been here countless times, in all its mutations, and from my briefest reference can place me in any room. I say the tower and you fly up to the tower. I say your room and you see yourself propped up in a certain bed regarding a strip of sea beneath a lowered shade.

It is—typical, anyway natural, that your mother linger, and that you must care for her; since we all have mothers and many of them linger, some stories overlap. Though we were a big family to share the work and worry, while you have only your own multiple personalities to fall back on: maid, cook, nurse, gardener, writer, young girl in love with the boy across the lake (who merges in your muddled mind with a local egret: the bird waits each morning until its feathers become a certain white with dawn, then flashes up into the air. It is the same white in the evening when it returns to its nest in the marsh; not the time of day but the quality of light). Is this not *exactly* how it is?

Two things have matured simultaneously: they say I should do nothing in the way of therapy, or that there is nothing to do; and a friend in Rome requires me to do his terrace. So I may go for a few months. By the time you get this I will be there, though I think I will call first, making all this superfluous.

(Mrs) *Imelda Marcos*

They had a rule against telephoning since it interrupted the letters, replaced or trashed them, and was expensive; though delicious, and if kept short and rare, occasionally preferable to the written word: pleasant to think some things were too inflammatory to write down. As a writer Matthew feared certain people might some day read them, who knew how? The Collected Letters of Matthew Black and Mark Valerian did not seem to be in the cards.

But sometimes direct contact and the twentieth century were required after all, though Matthew complained that his correspondents had gradually succumbed to the temptations of instant communication. But the telephone could be sudden and shocking. Alone in the house, he would be jangled and overloaded by the intrusion for hours afterward. It might ring at any moment, usually with bad news—another friend pronounced sick or dead—while letter-news was mellow, couched in some effort to soothe or amuse. What Mark liked about writing to Matthew was that he could say anything, personal or not, and Matthew—eccentric, even neurotic in certain ways—never took exception or offense. Some deep-seated confidence, intellectual confidence Mark thought, protected him from the usual defects of ego. Matthew was not vain, conceited, difficult, a liar, or lazy. His curiosity in anything could be aroused by the right inflection or approach. Perhaps because of the similarities of the two media, the letters and his writing, Matthew's main interests, his real topics, were the same in both: his yearning for love and affection, his mother, his apprehension of age. These were the things he might briefly allude to in the letters but which fundamentally obsessed him, in the way

Mark was obsessed by his family and now health, or what was left of it. So that they spoke and wrote to each other of these things in a kind of code.

Lake of Lost Souls Apr 14

Dear Mark,

Local egret darling? Muddled yes, but not re-duced to cruising the aviary. (Though you won't mind my pilfering the image.) Welcome to Rome! Apartment number thirty-eight. Read this on the west terrace. Filled with dread by the prospect of your flight—the last American to visit Europe in our time, escorted by enemy jets to starboard; the plane empty, chartered by a rich boyfriend. Is this not exactly how it was?

Myself have decided to head south instead when Sis comes, to Guadaloupe, with every-one else. No empty planes here. Or maybe Viechos. It's all the same beach and coral reef. I go only to scuba. The Caribbean is bearable under water. And safe.

Such good news re no need for therapy. The point is to put it off as long as possible. We are all v. good at that, n'est-ce pas? Mrs Ruggeri next door informs me that the trees I just planted as a screen between her and me will produce leaves which will drop on her lawn. We looked at each other for a long moment like two cows in a field. These people are hos-tile. Trees darling, not a hurricane fence, or a wall, but trees. The concept of privacy seems to have been carefully bred out of the Ruggeris.

And then the Challenger. Standing on our front lawns gaping at the smoky sky. Everything froze solid that night and we assumed they would cancel. Mrs Ruggeri insists an icicle pierced the booster skin. Now they say the crew capsule fell intact into the sea. Would a five-hundred-dollar parachute have saved them? I had thought that vaporization might send them into hyperspace and another dimension, but then there they were, hauled out of the sea like tuna . . .

I expect the usual floor plan, color swatches and rose petal samples.

From the terrace of the last apartment, sunsets at a certain point had been lost behind the looming dome of Chiesa Nuova; from here the eye was led to the point of it all—St Peter's, sitting stolidly through the situation as on the face of a huge clock. About as high as the Cape May tower, which now it replaced in Mark's mind, the empty terrace overlooked a heaving sea of orange tiles. Through the years he had redone a dozen such places. At some point in the sixties people had begun to pay him for this service. *Marco Valeriani: Vivaio.* He called himself a gardener although, if desired, you got the complete package, and anyway his gardens passed through his apartments like vines through a hollow tree. He did not like decorator: architect perhaps, down to his gun-metal tables made to order. From this present position—a large and completely naked terrace adjoining a large empty flat—he could see three others he had put together, and four more lurked amid the neighboring domes and altanas.

He had begun in the sixties by offering his services free of charge, by simply asking a friend to vacate her apartment for a few days. Astonishment had greeted a transformation that cost nothing. Objectivity, taste, placement, a certain chic. The houses of his friends became his showcases. He did several of these without charge, or at cost, with the stipulation that they mention his name when it came time for compliments. The rearrangement of furniture and the addition of a few plants and pots had then led to the reconstruction of a four-thousand-foot extravaganza in Parioli for la principessa della Scava. After that he had more work than he could handle because, to the princess, Mark represented an opportunity to redo not just her own place but those of all her friends, so that she need never again visit unattractive spaces for tea. It was more work than he could handle, and at this point he had gone back to Philadelphia. In the following decade—the seventies—he had done one or two terraces a year, then none.

Gardening was of course not what Mr Valerian had had in mind; to him it seemed an excuse to live an exotic, irresponsible life abroad. It was menial. My son the gardener was almost as bad as my son the homosexual. When, on a visit to Rome in the seventies, Mark showed his parents a recent installation rather like this one—overlooking all of Rome from a great height—they had understood some of it but not enough, in Mr Valerian's case, to offset his son's failure to own the situation itself. Yes, it was beautiful, but it belonged to someone else. Nor was it conceivable to his father that the profits from this occupation might allow him ever to buy such a place. Perhaps this was why Mark stepped back from success—not because he dreaded the work involved but because he had feared and distrusted what might come after: a life like his father's, the life of a businessman as opposed to the life of an artist. He no longer thought this way. He thought that most likely he was neither, to the degree that it could matter financially or artistically. Perhaps Mr Valerian was right. His life *was* exotic, irresponsible except to himself, most of all improvised. It had never seemed the point to make money or to choose one thing or profession over all others, since none of them particularly mattered. He had thought for a time he would like to write, and to rearrange words as he did furniture, but the closest he had come was in his letters to Matthew Black.

In the next few days he reassembled his crew—carpenter, plumber, electrician, tile man, Elda the maid—visited shopkeepers he had frequented over the years, bought huge garden vases and urns, oversaw the installation of an arbor on the terrace; bought furniture, pictures, prints, ordered curtains, linens. His client had money, and prices did not particularly matter; still he bargained judiciously, even harshly, since he was used to doing so, not to mention the question of fakes, and the next client who might not be so well-off.

23 April Rome

Matthew
    Have built an arbor worthy of Tiberius on
the roof, with twelve Doric columns (of wood)

painted a ruined putty color, supporting a combination of wisteria and grape vines growing out of enormous neoclassic urns. A fountain at one end, St Peter's obligingly framed and centered at the other. It will not look new. I've had enough dirt hauled up to sink the Bismarck and intend to sod it over with an American lawn. Don't ask who will mow it. Or with what. I will suggest sheep, as at the White House. I wonder what it all weighs. Since it is invisible it has been done without permits or scientific investigation. That is the secret here: *nascondere.* Hide it—Hide improvements, wealth, happiness, since to do otherwise is to tempt the gods and fate in the form of the Belle Arte committee, kidnappers and jealous neighbors with binoculars.

The apartment itself will be less interesting because I don't have the time or energy to do it all. This is carte blanche, but I can't see six months, which it would take to execute properly, so I'm doing an abbreviated version, falling back on blue and white, which you have seen my mother do at the beach, with her fat poles and white taffeta, plus black glass walls to cover the mess of centuries, good rugs, and drop-dead furniture of the fuck-you variety.

But I will tell you the difference here this time, and it is not just in my mind. Everyone is afraid of It. And of course in my case they are right. No more idle flirting with the workers. Just doesn't happen, though I don't know if this blockage is mutual or comes only from me. Perhaps I am suddenly old. I draw back from anything resembling a double entendre, whereas we all used to trip over them.

Up on the roof, in my future ruin. Later a moon, though not full. This place is very like the tower at home. I imagine the leathery sound of wings—not bats but an angel lighting down, naked, gorgeous. Since love made me ill, it should be that it cure me, and for that eventuality I have constructed a dense trellis in one corner where we could couple most angelically, unobserved.

Though I was right to come. I am well enough to pretend It does not exist. Everything is less real. This illusion makes me feel well. In the street you are not invisible as at home. So personal, I automatically look away, as if in fear of what might come next; though I am acclimating and now can stare down all but the most beautiful. Perhaps it is an advantage to know from my side that it can go nowhere; enough to be rendered visible again. What ghosts we are, over thirty, in the streets of America . . .

Open Desert Apr 29

Dear Mark

Understand the necessity of a letter waiting when you arrive, as I just did, back from New York (instead of Viechos) and where apparently I was expected. Not a stitch dropped. Was highly organized, saw at least one movie a day, three exhibitions, NO penises which is odd for New York. Ate Chinese, Indian, Korean, Japanese, Italian, French and Mexican. Ran into rather than saw people. For instance while in a bookstore la duchesse came in and we had lunch, so my cover was blown. How do they do it, day after day, with appointment books that look like medieval manuscripts and kitchens that never close? Went finally to a dinner party, just like in the old days, that I guess was in my honor, which was sweet, at which for five minutes we all spoke baby talk like Mrs Hamilton Fish in 1904. It is considered thank God bad manners to mention It at a dinner party (heretofore the death of same as we knew it) or that anyone new is ill. Herb was there and subdued us all with recent accomplishments until someone begged him to shut up. The entire city is career-crazed, since it's too dangerous to fuck. They work, cook, clean, garden, dress, and socialize with a vengeance. The result is San Francisco without the hills. After a week I came back.

Spent time with Sis who is so wonderful and easy, and who cleans up the mess of centuries as you say, and takes charge like a general and everything goes smoothly for a few days. I do nothing. Though Mum prefers the clutter I think and suspects that Sis is only doing it to keep sane in the face of—in the face of Mum. And Sis says it is odd to hear only the soundtrack of what was once a full-color spectacular by C B DeMille. She goes back to Nashville feeling that neatness is contentment, while Mum thinks that neatness may be simply a ticket home. And the cycle starts again. While I was in New York she threw away my entire collection of Mrs Smith pie plates.

Should have come there to you but was frightened, as everyone is, by what appears to be an Arab queen in jodhpurs and riding crop. I remember that Tiberius used to throw people from the top of Capri, which makes me *see* your arbor. Did you think to paint the crossbars blue? Probably not. I was last in Rome as a straight adolescent. I have changed; Rome I assume has not. (Coffee and biscotti on the north terrace!) Flying there seemed like risking World War III. I know that something would have happened. A swarthy young angel would have asked me to mind his bag while he went to the john. I know someone who was on the *Achile Lauro* and who spent the night before the hijacking in bed WITH ONE OF THE HIJACK-ERS. These things happen. In New York Ted asked me to do a piece on all of this, but more and more I want only to stay here by Lake Felicita and putter. Two days ago the world was gardening; today it is on a war-footing. If everyone would just get out of the mud and hire a good PR firm, the Palestinians would have their homeland TOMORROW, and 14th-century assholes everywhere would be out of a job. I want your reactions to all of this, asap, by fastest ships and ponies. The Press here acts-out so relentlessly and does not stop for something serious. Thank you for listening.

(Mrs) Edward R Murrow

Early mornings, rising in the empty, dusty, baronial flat, Mark made coffee and walked about, watering the plants, refining theoretical joins for the carpenter, making lists for the maid, sitting in the warming sun. *Le rondine* screamed through their morning feeding at a slanting moment equivalent to twilight. A nun resembling Queen Victoria wiped her lines to hang out dazzling Bernini folds on a convent roof. An odd bell pierced the evaporating mist. At a distance an old man tended his terrace vines. Tattered constreams lay across the naked blue sky. When the workers arrived he let them in and went down to look for perfect objects.

He felt certain that if he had stayed in Rome all these years he would not now be ill. None of his Italian friends was. Nor would they have easily supported the idea that Mark was. It never occurred to him to tell any of them; except one. Like everyone who spent time in Rome Mark knew a clairvoyant. Romans knew their clairvoyants the way they knew their tailors. Mark called and Romolo came to see the latest terrace, as he had seen them all over the years, not for the plants or the accomplishment but, as an artist, to sketch the view.

They spent the afternoon lying in the sun, watching people on the other terraces through binoculars. Romolo had brought his sketchbook and Tarot, and Mark watched him draw for hours, as a woman watches her lover do something that may at any moment be converted to sex. Since nothing in his life was sexual, other things became equivalent—any intimate act with another person in the absence of true intimacy was intimate. Romolo wore thick glasses, was short and small-boned, had for years worn a costume of faded blue denim in free association with the blithe informalities of Americans in the sixties, but also as a comment on the magic of blue; with many rings and bracelets that served, one could see, as amulets as much as cross-gender reference and decoration. Each piece had its history and use, its own magic. He spoke softly, almost in a whisper, with a gentleness that constructed a private world beyond that which was obvious to everyone.

Finally, over the cards, after Mark had first explained the situation, the future looked complicated, even annoying, but ultimately nearly as bright as ever. It was the first time anyone—doctors, people he had told, friends, family—had not privately, automatically assumed he would die. Casually dropping the cards in threes, Romolo spoke softly but confidently in terms of a cure. In itself vague, the dates of its accomplishment uncertain; but a cure, or at least defeat of the disease. Mark was astonished and blinked back sudden tears of gratitude. He realized he had not felt this momentary lightness since the day they had said he was ill.

"It is now in your spleen and liver," Romolo said. "At a certain point you might have pissed it out, by drinking great quantities of water. A shame . . ."

The cure would not be for everyone, but for *"certi individuali,"* Mark among them. "It happened at an orgy *sul cavallo di* 'eighty-one, 'eighty-two"—over New Year's of 1982. Mark could not distinguish this event from any of several in memory. A man he had known, and been with once before, was the carrier, though he himself had not subsequently become ill. Even now, Romolo said, Mark might find this person at a certain bar not far from a circular piazza in New York, at the end of a long street on which there was an important hotel: a tall man, dark, perhaps Latino, with a short name that ended in *ch*. Romolo wrote on his sketch pad, RESCH.

Mark suggested Rich.

"*Non sono sicuro*. Perhaps. But in any case it was sex. *Non ti hanno avvelenato*." They didn't poison you.

There had been many theories. Some believed the Russians or the CIA, or Idi Amin, had made a genetic mistake with germ warfare; or that a massive effort in Africa to wipe out smallpox with a live vaccine had activated the virus, or that the American conservative right had purposely dropped something into the pool at the Everard Baths in New York City. Others maintained that gamma globulin shots administered to cover a hepatitis epidemic among gay men in the seventies had been tainted by infected plasma collected in Haiti and Africa. This would account for the prevalence of the disease in the U.S. gay population. In Mark's case, his liver had already been weakened by hepatitis, for which he had been given *two* gamma globulin shots. He had often immersed himself in the ancient pool at the Everard; had attended orgies in New York City. Whatever the epidemiology, it had found him. Rich.

Romolo rearranged the cards again and went on. "*Ci sera della radioattivitá . . .*"

"Radiation, for me?"

"*Per tutti*," Romolo said, and shrugged his shoulders. For everyone. "*Non ti fara male*." He looked down again. The cure would take some time. An adjustment of the dosage would be necessary to protect the kidneys. By 1988 Mark would be cured, though his doctors would consider him well even before that. Yes, he would again be able to make love. Sooner than he thought. Why not? He would be as good as new.

"In the meantime you must not be depressed. It is in the mind as in the body . . . Push it from your mind, with energy, and it will leave the body. Not just the cure, but your energy will defeat it." It was as Vita had said, something within himself.

Little enough to go on—the word of a *mago*—but he was exhilarated for days. He did not mention it to anyone, not even in his next letter to Matthew, to whom he told everything; because it seemed, considering the source, that these ideas might be subject to change, and that often change itself was subject to odd, unknown, unknowable superstitions.

☆

1 May Rome

(Matthew)

Today everything is closed: the works, and everyone off. The nuns, you remember, used to make a scene on May Day (this year we're celebrating a Russian toxic event) with a procession into church, special flowers, singing and carrying on. I remember especially "O Mary, we crown thee with blossoms today/Queen of the Angels, Queen of the May . . ."

The radio says the Chernobyl cloud is loaded with plutonium and totally dangerous, but is expected to blow north. England has gone indoors, all the streets of Europe are empty. The milk in Finland is not recommended. The weather here has been shit, though the sun comes and goes to remind us. All over Rome my terraces are greening up and blooming. Jasmine (rinko sperma, yum yum) is in bud, weeds are in their flowering, presentable stage, when you don't want to pull them out of the Piranesi but should. Roses have already made a first show, while at home you are still in the forsythia–weeping-willow stage. This time my client is prepared to winter-wrap, so I am free to do things like palms and banana trees, which help give a terrace that Suddenly Last Summer look, of the near-mad. The sod was lain yesterday and the effect is eerie, more like wall-to-wall than lawn, not quite real because of the seams; but wait. The arbor has the look of a temple in a country glade. What is the use of beauty without mystery? you ask. To stun.

Yesterday afternoon went to a movie house that used to foster sex in the balcony in the old days; simply because I had to see that look in a man's eye, and preferably get a glance at some privates. Someone groped me in the dark, and suddenly I was afraid. I fled, even though I would never have done anything but look or lightly touch for an instant. I remember the horror, before I was ill, of hearing about someone out there anyway, or at the baths. I wanted to see that it still happened, was all still there. But how awful. Too little left of what we once thought was limitless. I think to be well again would be to find it still is limitless, as something you qualify for . . . So true, signorina. Is that your real hair?

Ask Mrs Ruggeri if she would prefer a nice stand of wild bamboo instead of your well-behaved trees. I have seen whole towns disappear in its path. Have you considered ailanthus, the rat of trees? The crossbars ARE blue, thank you. There is in the air the sense of impending arrival, impending departure, impending something. I am thinking about a sprinkler system for the lawn on the roof and assume all this to be an enactment of the construction of my own grave. The symbol of something similar. My sister Vita would know in an instant.

Reactions to what is happening are vague. Recently nonparticipatory in Civics and World events. Seems preoccupied.

Mark's teacher (Mrs)

Every morning on the terrace, with a cup of coffee in his hand, he put Cape May in mind, where for a moment lay the image of sparkling sun on the water, a sharp horizon, the empty beach, before fading into the intricate ocher angles of Roman rooftops. His watering and arranging, his obsessive buying and collecting struck him now as an effort to offset or reconstruct or revivify his feelings for the beach house. As the weeks passed, as the spaces developed, the sensation of a connection between the two places was heightened by a developing similarity. The *salotto* looked like the blue room, which spatially it had resembled to begin with, and in it he felt the same momentary calm of recollection and recognition—an association with his mother. He had meant it as a reference to her, and when the white taffeta curtains went up over a duplication of her huge bedroom window, he felt he had done something she would have liked. Instead of for his client, a Milanese hotelkeeper, he had done everything here for Margaret, as a construction of the sort of place he assumed she might now occupy in heaven, and where she was supremely content. In this Roman flat, far from a world she had seldom in life ever left, he dreamed of her often—brief fragmentary dreams that came like messages, communications he was meant to decipher and remember. She held him while he wept, smiling at his sadness, and meaning him to know by this smile that if not soon it would someday be over. On a station platform in a strange city, she was dressed for traveling, with long gloves and a small suitcase. "Darling," she said, "it's you. Just in time to help me find a seat." She would be going on; he not. Then, in her own apartment somewhere, which none of them had seen— lovely spaces filled with familiar objects; all of them invited for dinner and Margaret herself happy, in serene control, showing him the place, their photographs on a gueridon, here where she lived alone.

He awoke. These dreams meant he was not to die. She had appeared because she knew that without hope he would not get well, that if he died now he would make bad company, endlessly sad at the unfairness of life, its shortness: filled with anger, unable to rest.

He came up to the terrace and watched the sun rise, heard the early discreet single bells; the birds. The sky colored, the sun came up over the rail on a line with the arbor columns as through the rose window of a long church nave. These religious/pagan echoes, harnessing the sun's importance, orientation, seemed to anchor the place in time, in the particular live moment, as if it had always been. Its beauty was wounding, like a pair of perfect breasts or fierce eyes. The lemon light, turning orange, struck with the delicacy of chimes. It could not have seemed more lonely. He didn't believe Margaret was in heaven or that she had not, four years before, simply ceased to be. But her heaven might be his fantasies for her, as was his. The point was that they overlap somehow. This gave comfort: that they be together, that he not be alone.

3 May Fla-Fla

Dear Mark,

The Russians darling. Not a word, as if they had simply farted and hoped no one would notice or identify. Isn't one supposed to say excuse me and light a fucking match? But no. Such swine. Two dead. Two *thousand* dead. Boo Boo Payne's picnic heinously ruined. Flowers that glow. Cows that can't stop weeping. Enormous emeralds lying on the ground. Hollow zucchini. Fabulous sunsets. Everyone in huge Mylar hats. So many ways for mankind to screw up. Shouldn't there be a meltdown every day? And is this the first, or just the first we know about? Who needs actual war when dealing with ignorance and incompetence on SUCH a scale. Mum heard the news on TV and said, "Is that

a joke?" I said it wasn't and she said, "Good."
"Good?" I asked. "Is a toxic cloud over Europe good?" "My dear," she said, "there's a
toxic cloud over the entire planet. It's called
Ignorance."

Got something very strange in the mail, from
a gay group in Austin that is raising funds for
a private space program, to find a livable planet
to colonize. A gay planet darling. Like the Pines
I guess only bigger and not so hard to get to.
The reason being that if we don't get off Earth
we will die—this being the real significance of
the Government's space program: not enough
room. So I wrote back saying yes, sign me up
and here's my check for twenty-five dollars.
Of course you think of Challenger blowing up
and wonder if highly organized queens can do
better.

Sending you a friend, who like you is unintimidated by what might be in the baggage
compartment, who is passing through Rome.
You will like each other. His name is William
Mackey. Will give him your number unless you
call to say you have utterly taken the veil.

☆

They said on Italian TV that the Cloud would go the
other way, toward the North Pole; but over the weekend it blew down to southern Europe. It was said
radiation levels were weak but they did not sound
certain about it. Most vegetables were condemned and

destroyed. No more artichokes. Ironically, corgettes were all right and would continue to be available. Everyone ate bananas and wanted iodine from the chemists. Milk was dumped. By Sunday evening the Cloud had not dispersed, though neither was it visible anywhere to the naked eye. The streets of Rome were empty but no more so, Mark thought, than seemed normal for a weekend at this time of year. The sunsets were fabulous, but they always were. Perhaps they tended more toward vermilion. He had the idea that a mild dose of radiation might be good in his case. Romolo had said it would not do him harm, and anyway here was something else that did not seem quite real. The birds came and went as usual. He would have liked to ask Romolo about all this, but he had gone to Milan to mount an exhibition of paintings.

His client was due the following week and Mark pushed to get things ready. Enzo was middle-aged and well-to-do, having made a great success of a small hotel in Milan. He had the natural taste of an Italian his age but none of the stinginess, and depended on Mark to help him create a certain impression in Rome; something to match the *figura* he cut in the North. He was not content with being fashionable. Just now it was not fashionable to be fashionable. It was, in Milano, not the hour- or minute-, but the second-hand that people watched. The flat had been extensively rebuilt some years before, the kitchen had changed places with the dining room, a bedroom with a bath, a bath with a hall—a reshuffling so general it had taken some time for details of the new arrangement to appear as what they were, or were not. Mark's job was to refinish the last part of the process—the internal veneer: the walls, furniture, rugs, curtains; and of course the terrace.

Now the walls had been replastered, painted, and waxed, one room lined completely with bookcases and soon with books. A bathroom had been mirrored. The ceiling in the dining room was polished brass, the walls in the foyer black glass. A number of architectural details had been carefully picked out in *faux marbre*. Rugs were down. A black ebony piano had come through the new window by crane. A system of lighting that Mark himself could only characterize as smart-ass was complete, though some of the pictures and objects to be lighted had not yet arrived, among them a huge *ottocento* canvas for which he had paid four million lire, but which he believed to be worth ten times that. This huge painting of the Pantheon, measuring six feet across, would carry the salotto, though there remained the interesting question of who had painted it. Enzo had been asked to wait for it to be cleaned and hung before making his next visit. Both events were planned for the following week.

Elda, the Roman woman who cleaned for Mark, was constantly red-faced from the effort to keep up. For fifteen years she had come to clean whatever apartment Mark was occupying. He brought her gifts, scarves, perfume; had helped her son find a job. She seldom came through the door without a sweet she had made, or a pile of his laundry done by hand. She saw he was ill and said nothing, since this was what he wanted, but babied him as she would have any man within her range; asked him if he had napped, eaten, felt well; all the solicitations of a relative. She worked in a luxury hotel nearby; his was the only private house she cleaned. Her husband of thirty years had recently run off with a thirty-two-year-old. Elda had seen them together. The husband had been incapacitated by the great influenza epidemic after the War. She had supported him and their son all this time by working in the hotel. Now the swine had taken their money and bought an apartment for his young slut. "*E va bé . . . Che si puo fa?*" She said it often, but in her heart there was murder, and automatic tears in her eyes. After Mark found her son the job she was ready to clean for him until she dropped; Mark in her mind fell somewhere between husband and son, brother perhaps; she enjoyed the exotic and unexpected. She loved watching the changes that took place in the fabulous apartments he had called her to over the years, one after the other.

Matthew's friend telephoned and Mark invited him over. Matthew had minimized the man's attractions. William Mackey's sunniness, his looks, his show of pleasure at the apartment and its views were threatening. Mark did not feel qualified for all this. After Bill left, Mark burst into tears and slapped a banana leaf in the face. Some hours later, Mackey called again, as if in fact it had gone well, and asked if they might have dinner. Mark was old enough, lonely enough to snatch at the reprieve, and they met in Piazza Navona. In a restaurant nearby he made a lighthearted toast to Bill's trip and then, impulsively, deciding it was all he had to give, and as if it would explain everything, he told him he was ill.

"I'm sorry . . . So am I," Bill replied.

"What do you mean?"

"I have it, too. I was diagnosed a year ago." He lifted his glass again, and Mark touched it with his.

"Does Matthew know?" Mark asked.

"Of course."

"But you don't look sick. You're so perfect looking."

Bill blushed and looked away, looked back. "The apartment is beautiful," he said, changing the subject. "It looks finished."

"It is."

"Then what?"

"I'll go back to Philadelphia for a while. Or Cape May."

"What's Cape May?"

"We have a beach house there."

"That must be something," Bill said, and took a sip of wine.

"Yes." They smiled. Mark started to cry.

"Mark, it's okay."

"I'm a mess," he said, looking down, then wiping his eyes.

"Who isn't?"

The waiter came and Mark straightened up. They ordered.

"Does Matthew know about you?" Bill asked.

"Yes. I think he's been playing matchmaker-nurse."

"I don't mind," Bill said with a sly, devastating smile.

After dinner they walked slowly through the streets. Mark took his arm, as they do there, feeling the hard bulk of the bicep. On the roof terrace they touched hands, held each other, did not kiss.

"What are the rules, do you think?" Mark asked.

"No idea. Sick is sick, I guess. How much worse could it be?"

"Just hold me. That's all I want," Mark said. "I can't imagine anything else."

"Oh, I can . . . Don't be frightened, Mark. It's all right."

They did kiss, a soft, sweet kiss. And in an angle of the terrace enclosed by dense trellis, as anticipated, they made love.

In the morning light they showed each other the spots on their bodies. Except for two on his neck, Bill's were confined to his left arm and leg. All that remained on Mark were small scars from six or seven lesions that had been removed, and others on the bottom of his right foot that he intended to take care of at home.

"Why did you have them removed?" Bill asked, touching Mark's foot the way Dr Thompson did, fearlessly, with tactile interest.

"They seemed like little factories to me. I shut them down. No one agrees."

With sheets around their shoulders and cups of coffee, they went up to the terrace and sat where they had made love the night before, watching the birds dart in and out of a milky blue mist. Farther reaches of the city slowly came into focus. A single bell rang out with a clarity lacking in everything else . . . eight, nine, ten, eleven. You could see in the sound a little man in robes with a hammer . . . twelve, thirteen, fourteen.

"This is it," Bill said. "Perfection, two thousand years later."

"And very bad alone," Mark added. "No matter how beautiful."

"Never mind that," he said. "You aren't alone. I'll stay as long as you like."

"I'm not easy," Mark said.

"You appear to be a piece of cake. Let's just see. No predictions. No promises . . . I'm grateful to Matthew," Bill said. "This was a humane act—further evidence of his genius with gay men. Though he probably did it on a whim, because we found ourselves in the same city with the same friend."

"—And the same disease," Mark added. "It was too coincidental for a writer to let pass."

The sun was clearing the mist. Mark let the sheet fall from his shoulders. He felt warm. It was at this point they received the heaviest dose of radiation from the Cloud; in this case a combination of Iodine 131, Strontium 90, and Cesium 137, in unknown quantities.

"Is there someone in New York?" Mark asked.

"There was. He got It first . . . Fred was a few years older than me." Bill looked away, over the rooftops. "I couldn't go through that again."

"You won't have to," Mark said. "I have no intention of dying."

"I'm sorry. That sounded odd."

"I know. But I'm not going to die, not from this anyway. Everyone expects it. It's automatic. But you can't let yourself. You just say no."

"No."

"That's right."

"No, no, and no."

*   *   *

Bill postponed his departure for two days. "I want you to come with me," he said. "You're done here. Let me take you away from all this"—he waved his hand—". . . this squalor."

"Enzo is due in three days."

"It'll wait," Bill said. "Or you could meet me. In Florence . . . No, Venice. We'll meet in Venice, next week."

They were constantly touching. Mark already ached for him, although he recognized this as an abstract feeling—as much for the excitement of having someone as for Bill himself.

"You realize it's a trip without vegetables. Everything is condemned. Does Venice without vegetables make sense?"

They heard Elda's key in the door. Mark jumped up and dressed, leaving Bill in the bed. Elda wanted to know how Mark was. His face was red. Did he have a fever?

"No, I'm fine. It's just that . . ."

"That what? What is it?" She put her hand to her heart which was still pounding from the stairs, but also because these things worried her. Everything worried her.

"I have a guest. From America. *Un amico.* He's inside." In short sentences he was totally authentic. It was all a native had to hear to react like a Roman.

"Is that all? Good . . . Can I get you something? Do you want a coffee?"

He wanted to say he was in love, but couldn't, though she might not have been surprised, wounded or offended, since it was Mark. He wanted to share it with her. He couldn't be sure. She might think, even after all these years, that it was no business of hers; or that like her husband he was running off with someone, which he was.

"No, *niente*."

"*Quanto e bello*," Elda said when she saw him. "*E un angelo*." Mark thought this meant she knew Bill's beauty was the basis for their friendship, that this was well worth it and rather natural. The least he could have said, to excuse the difference in their ages—even to account for the fact that in an apartment with two glamorous guest rooms they were sharing the same bed—was that Bill was like a *frattellino*. But out of respect for Elda he did not. It didn't matter. The whole preoccupation was a projection of Bill's eventual reception in Cape May, which meant not that Mark wondered what his family would think, he didn't care what they thought, but that it was clear, even now, he intended to take him home.

Lying in bed beside him, he wondered at the sudden rejuvenation of his sex life, after two years of depressed celibacy during which it had seemed he would never again so much as kiss. In place of real sex he had begun mentally to catalogue old encounters from the past, as many as he could remember over a period of twenty years, starting with when he had come out at twenty-two. Of all of them he could recall perhaps fifteen episodes and these only for some vital detail, some fragmentary moment that had stuck in the mind. His generation had made love in great numbers, not from a sense of disobeying rules or smashing traditional morality but because moral, social reasons for abstinence no longer obtained against this sudden bursting of physical beauty and exuberance into their lives; it was the result of natural forces magnified by great numbers, into a phenomenon. Tandem notions of attachment and sex were meticulously, scrupulously disentangled. For them as for no other generation, it could be either, instead of both or neither one.

But when he made love with Bill he wondered each time if in fact this could be the last of so many; and he would look at the handsome face with a feeling of gratitude and apprehension, alternating appreciation and doubt. For it did not seem possible he would have this chance again. And the addition of this painful sensation, that each time was the last, made sex something at once precious and desperate, like a last meal or parting glance. He had faced the idea of abstinence, and the dire lack of love (which was different) and had lived with it for some time, making this reprieve all the sweeter. But having enjoyed an earlier career as a sexual athlete he knew not to expect or require their coupling to be, automatically, romantically binding. Life now was more complicated than when such ideas were considered naïve, unreasonable. They both were ill, however, not just Mark. Bill's celibacy was also real, also momentarily suspended. Nor could it be said that the sadness, the poignancy of their sex brought abandon or thoughtlessness. Each of them held back, with the collected, considerate reserve of elderly lovers who worry for each other's hearts or brittle bones. They kissed, but not so often or deeply as both would have liked. They used condoms. They used their eyes whereas formerly each of them would have simply devoured. With the certainty of illness, one thing was gone: fear. This was the irony—that they who knew themselves to be dangerous to others, and thus to themselves, seemed safe with each other. It was in itself automatically a strong attachment.

15 May Rome

Dear Matthew,

The delay is your fault, Matchmaker to the stars. We both want you to know that it worked, or seems to have worked, and that I at least am rather in love, which is so ironic and odd, as you of all people will understand. Bill called and came over, it was awful for reasons I won't go into; then he called again and it all came out—about me, about him, about It—which made of course all the difference. Stayed a few extra days here with me. Left this morning, giving me at last a moment to think and write to you, who are all good and deserving of all our love. Have I failed to say that I am meeting him in Venice in four, no three days? At the Danieli, for tea. In the meantime he has gone to Florence, I await Enzo (client from Milan) who I assume will cream and froth and exude Italian perfumes at the sight of his new house in the sky. Bill likes it, which is all that matters.

Imagine that you should perform this service for an old friend . . . after all these years, like some hidden unexpected use for what had been thought a totally useless object. When Elda saw him she thought he had been lowered from the sky on piano wires, as did I. When she's nervous, which is always, she runs her fingers through her hair, and I thought this time she was going to snatch herself bald. Won't rhapsodize since you know what he looks like, but I think he is so beautiful, so cool and calm and sweet-smelling and brave. And there's the mush part—which perhaps you can imagine, perhaps not, being from the South; when we both thought this sort of thing over for the Duration. It is the greatest relief to feel for a change that your kiss will not this time destroy Cincinnati.

In the meantime it has been scary with the CLOUD, which comes and goes. They say it is gone, the danger is past, but all the women say otherwise, all the cats are ga-ga, lying on the tops of cars in a stupor, not moving when you pass. Today there was supposed to be more of it but the sky clear and vividly blue all day. It is of course, being only radioactive steam, totally invisible. At the moment there's a rally taking place in Piazza Navona from which I hear angry stentorian wisps on the wind. Both B and I have had terrible headaches all week but he says he has them a lot, too, anyway, and we can't be sure if it's us or the Russians. A friend who works for a big pharmaceutical here says it has all been exaggerated, he says they must themselves take extra care because they work around radioactivity anyway; that the air is okay, though not the veg, milk or cheese. All livestock stopped at the border, or sent to lesser hotels. It is time to leave Rome, clearly; past time. However Venice with Bill is the wrong direction. Nevertheless. In the luxury of the Danieli I will convince him to come to Cape May. You know about his friend dying. He may not be ready for what I absolutely want, now that I have had a taste. He's been gone only two hours and I miss him beyond explanation. A nervous feeling, not pleasurable, but not not. Do you think any of this is wise? What do I do, *feel*, if it doesn't work out? Who knows what he really thinks? Headaches or not I've been happy this week. Could the radiation, at these low levels, not have done us some good? Share the fantasy.

(Mrs) John Huston

Enzo and the huge painting of the Pantheon arrived simultaneously, creating something of a bottleneck in the hall. The drama of this enormous canvas was gripping. Here was splash. Here was glamour. Enzo suddenly wished his Milan apartment could look the same.

"It can, but not this year," Mark replied.

Enzo wondered, after a while, if the piano was where it should be. Mark said everything was precisely where it should be, but that he, Enzo, could do what he liked—including heaping it all in a pile in the center of the room—as long as he waited until he, Mark, was out the door.

"But where are you going?" Enzo asked, incredulous and dazed.

"To Venice. I'm in love."

"But can't she wait? We have things to discuss. The accounts. The details . . ."

"He, not she. As for the accounts, it's all in here." He presented a folder of bills and invoices. "You owe me thirty million lire, and I would like a check in that amount within the next thirty seconds, otherwise, for details, this vase hits that wall, and this piano goes out that window."

"Marco, be serious . . ."

"The check. It's done. I have a train to catch."

Venice was empty of tourists, except for large groups of German widows who, having survived the cruelest, most demanding generation of husbands ever, were unfazed now by vague concepts of radiation—which, unlike dirt, could not be seen or smelled and therefore to them was not real. They wandered about looking up, as if culture dwelt in the upper stories, while waiters stood idle before empty, perfectly prepared restaurants, eying them as they passed. A single group of Teutonic ladies was all a restaurant needed; waste at the end of each day was tremendous since no one trusted the vegetables, and handsome waiters wooed them as if they were young girls, with smiles and flourishes of their towels. The *vaporetti* for similar reasons were empty, and hundreds of empty gondolas, rafted together, formed an undulating mat of black shapes bobbing and rippling halfway across the Grand Canal. What the Russians had killed with their Cloud, besides the vegetables, was tourism.

Bill Mackey, in blue, stood outside the Danieli. Smiling, they encircled each other's waist with an arm, in a half-turn that let them face the sun-dazzled water. Nothing had changed in four days or five hundred years. They went up to the room that Bill had converted to a double at the front, a cavernous place with pelmets and swags and a huge bed four feet off the floor. They showered, and since Mark was more than tired, napped in each other's arms; then awoke and dressed, after dark, and went down in search of dinner, being now ravenous. Afterwards they hired a gondola from the quay, choosing a handsome face out of the waiting *gondolieri*, and set out through the back canals, facing each other at first. Then the night air, cooler still on the water, hit; and Bill moved to sit beside him, under the blanket, with the rhythmic sounds and leanings of the gondolier over their heads.

"*Potrei cantare, si vi piace.*" Gliding through watery moonlit halls. "He wants to sing," Mark whispered.

"Let him, he's cute." Bill smiled encouragingly up at the oarsman. In a sweet supple tenor the young gondolier hit a high note that flew off in the dark, floating out like a bird down the narrow canal. An echo at first, but from another gondola somewhere in front of them, returned, slightly muffled and distant, as from offstage, and with a flourish appended to the end; which then their gondolier again took up, thrillingly. Drifting closer in the dark they embroidered each other's phrases until, passing in a canal so narrow that for a moment they stood side by side, the sound amplified by high damp walls, their two voices merged as in the climax of a lovely aria. Seated in the other gondola a man and a woman laughed and applauded broadly, smiling and waving, until mercifully they were swept away. Over Bill and Mark, their oarsman took up something familiar quietly, nearly to himself, and they glided around another corner into the wide silver reach of the Grand Canal.

In the room watching water shadows on the twenty-foot ceiling, Mark lay against Bill's chest wondering at the unlikelihood of the situation, the place, the company—he who sexually, romantically, had given himself up for lost.

"How perfect this would be if we weren't . . ."

"Yes," Bill said after a long moment.

"Do you think we shouldn't push it?" Mark asked finally.

"I notice you like questions that imply their own outrageous logic . . . I'm supposed to go to Paris, then London and home. Will you come with me? Traveling alone . . . This trip . . ." Bill went on, then stopped. "Fred left me all his money. But I'm not used to being alone."

He pushed open the doors to the balcony and rushed back to bed. Sunlight flooded in. Through the balustrade the Adriatic gleamed and shimmered under an empty blue bell. Hundreds of years of mornings seemed flung down in stripes of light aslant the crooked floor. In a moment someone would bring in enormous *cappuccinos*.

"I want to see the Horses of San Marco," Mark exclaimed. "And feed the pigeons, see the clock strike . . ."

". . . Buy rubbers," Bill added. "You ate the last of them last night. But judging from the numbers I see floating in the canals . . ."

"Those are not rubbers. They are Long Island whitefish, brought here by Ben Franklin."

"Does that mean you're rich?" Mark said.

"Does what mean I'm rich?"

" 'All Fred's money,' " he quoted.

"I'm not in your league, but I'm not indigent."

"My league? I have Enzo's thirty million lire. That's it. Except that, in certain years, I'm an heiress ... What did Fred do?"

"He owned a restaurant. When he got sick he sold it, for rather a lot. Then there's a cooperative in New York, and a cabin in western Mass."

"Darling."

"I know. Wait till you see."

"Between us, there's rather a lot of real estate."

They went through the Doge's Palace, took another gondola ride, had lunch at *da Raffaello* where, because of the Cloud, the *risotto alla pescatore* was in demand. However they both had headaches and were tired enough to sleep through the afternoon and evening. Later they ordered up, and watched TV in the room. Mark wanted to rearrange the furniture but most of it was too heavy to shift. They did not precisely have sex but they did not precisely not. Mark liked simply holding Bill's genitals in his hand.

"You can't hold it too tight," Mark whispered, "or it will fly away ..."

Sunday they decided to stay another night; then Bill would go on. Mark would fly home from Milan after cashing the check at Enzo's bank. Exporting this kind of money—twenty thousand dollars' worth—was illegal and certainly would mean prosecution if discovered. The only alternative would be spending it. Monday morning he saw Bill off at the train station, then flew to Milan. In the afternoon Enzo met him to see about the check. Dogs at the airport were trained to sniff out bombs, not cash, and he was let through without incident.

15 May Cape May

Dear Matthew

They honeymooned in Venice of course, the most romantic city in the world after Gainesville. The discretion of gondoliers who have seen it all for centuries. When Bill put his arm around me against the chill I shivered with gratitude at the sense of romantic legitimacy. These small rebellions are more thrilling than rock throwing and slogans on the barricades, and more effective since they take place in the heart of enemy territory: I thought, will he stop and tip us into the canal? Do even gondoliers draw the line? This one didn't. Instead he sang for us while we cuddled closer and I fell the rest of the way in love. Love is half-theatrics—the right song at the perfect moment.

And then what? How do you follow Venice? Do you trudge off to Frankfurt for the sausage? Paris, in this case. But Paris without me, I thought, might almost be equal to Venice with. So I came home.

You must tell me everything. About Bill. About the late Fred. The ruined lives, tragedy, scenes

in the hospital, cemetery. Ashes. In the old days
we came to each other with elaborate pasts, usually in a bar or at some kind of developing
orgy. Now we present letters of introduction
from mutual friends. Total unsuitability—to
make a dowager lady blanch—has been replaced
by dowries that each make bitter little stories.
The great irony is that this romance is suitable
only because of It. If it were not in both of
us, or even neither of us, fear would have prevented everything outright. Perhaps this is not
mere irony. To be ill in his company, in his arms
(forgive me) is to be well in relation to each
other. How could either of us get through without something to go on? We are ill but It does
not mean what it did, day to day. All depression gone. Not so frightening, not so real.

Being back in Cape May is not enough, or
wouldn't be if I weren't waiting for him. Something about to happen is what was lacking. This
morning he called from London and said he
was constantly pointing things out to bewildered
ladies of another generation. Will send a car
and driver to meet him at the airport and, since
local chauffeurs are not gondoliers, will wait
for him here. Am already waiting. Then, next
Sat, Tess and Vita and my father and Aunt
Rose will be here, to see me, to meet Bill, although I haven't told them yet about him. They
will absorb him like a spilled drink before my
eyes. They will secretly count themselves lucky
that he speaks English and does not look like.

Othello, or Desdemona, though they would absorb that too. The liberal families of gay men must be the adaptable salt of the earth . . .

☆

Bill arrived exhausted and was put to bed, in the back bedroom downstairs where it was dark for naps. Mark watched him sleep, watched him slide between the semblance of life and the semblance of death, which is chiefly a matter of stillness. He wondered if Bill would let him love the way he had loved a boyhood friend he hadn't seen in thirty years, or his dog, or two or three men over the years—none of whom, except the dog, had managed to love Mark in return. Sometime later, in the dark, Bill called out Fred's name, and Mark, who had also fallen into a deep sleep, with a start had to recollect the name, the company, the country. He thought, I am what's left of Fred. Instead of wanting something different, Bill wanted, like any widower, a reconstruction of what he had lost, with of course a different ending. This time, Mark thought, they would move around the world from place to place like the duke and duchess of Windsor; and with his heart aching with love, he fell back to sleep.

PART

THREE

Three lesions on Mark's foot had seemed to defy the idea of surgery, being deeply set in the sole in two cases; a fat bubble, like a blood blister on the heel, in the third. Before Rome Dr Thompson had suggested radiation, but not until the lesions matured. Now, day by day the first week in Cape May, with wonder, Mark watched them fade. The bubble emptied itself and flattened, leaving a scarcely noticeable discoloration under the callus on the heel. Others, though less changed, seemed diminished. Headaches gone. This might mean nothing or everything.

Bill slept through much of his first two days, too jet lagged to register substantive changes or effects from the Cloud, and merely tired. Sleepy still he walked about the house with a cup of tea, sitting here and there, looking at the spaces, the views, the water, dunes, lighthouse, the cabochon pond. "Here's another place to sit," he exclaimed, settling into a window seat with his tea. Because of his feelings for Mark, because of the place itself, he saw and responded to it rather in the same way—as a huge, romantic anachronism, a luxurious pile, being so much itself as to evoke uniform reactions: awe, pride or envy, delight, intense domesticity. Bill, who had been too exhausted at first, waked to it gradually as if room to room, the spaces created around him in an expanding sequence. "My God . . ." Mark heard him exclaim on the second day. "There's another floor up here . . ."

But far from fading lesions, Bill found two new smudges—probably the effects of such fatigue—on his arm; and the idea diminished that somehow their exposure to the Cloud in Rome had been beneficial. Neither of them had the energy to accomplish anything beyond the immediate simplicities of the garden or a walk around the pond; and every afternoon they slept in each other's arms for two, even three hours. They went to town only for food and newspapers, were in bed asleep by eleven. Mark put it down for Matthew.

　　. . . the feeling that while I would be content with him anywhere, enthralled even, I am thoroughly blissed by his reaction to the house—and, I must admit, by the house's reaction to him. How dotty darling to think a house cares.

　　Tomorrow the world arrives, my sisters and aunt, plus various nieces, my oldest nephew who is Tessa's lifeguard son and therefore a local deity. He and the others and their friends, for whom the summer does not start for two more weeks, inhabit their own world, though the older girls use corridors between the two, theirs and ours, separate worlds that overlap only over food, location and transportation. Otherwise we know nothing of each other, other than what we are told. Being an uncle. The occasion for the adults is to see me but also, unbeknownst, to meet Bill, about whom so far they know nothing. For I think the fewer automatic preconceptions the better. The question is, do we tell them that he is also ill? or do we not? Or do we wait until later? Nothing, I see, has much changed: it is still a question of coming out of the closet with something vile about yourself. You follow? The secretly ill, not just because of the evil associations everyone makes, the fear harbored or suppressed; but because being ill is itself in such bad taste. You don't yourself feel right about it, why should others? Making a double burden for Bill: they would otherwise be disposed to like and accept him immediately, since it is my wish, and since on Christmas Eve they feel guilty when I go home alone and they divide themselves equally among three trees. I will finish this when the dust settles . . .

On Saturday Tessa and Aunt Rose arrived together rather early, or as if together but in separate cars. Logistics by car were as nothing to Rose, Mrs. Valerian's widowed sister-in-law, who lived some distance from Tessa, and whose large automobile, like her small tidy house, was maintained mint. Now they came through the door with bags of groceries and food—Rose's *melanzana*, for instance, a cake Tessa had thought to bake. Bill was presented, as something of a surprise, their having thought of the weekend as being as usual just them. Tessa had this time brought the baby, little Margaret, or Mara as they called her, and a young mother's helper, a contemporary of Tessa's teenage daughter whose own activities, nonetheless, defied the interruptions of a baby sister. Little Mara looked up at the tall stranger—a man—and gripped the tailored bodice of her sensible traveling doll, Estelle.

"This is Uncle Mark's friend," Tessa explained, as if to excuse the hugeness in the hall. Bill made himself smaller, in a crouch, and gently touched Mara's tummy with a fingertip; she smiled at the kindness, and Tessa, to herself, again admired her child's clothes. "Carol will take you to the beach, honey, if you like," she said over Bill's lowered head. "Would you like that?" Carol began immediately to turn toward various doorways off the hall, indicating a teenager's willingness, a teenager's inability. "It's through there," Tessa indicated. The differences in Mara's life, as from Tessa's at her age, were defined in terms of the solitary, as opposed to the sibling, child. It seemed Tessa meant Mara never to be actually alone.

Tessa had recently lost as much as forty pounds—legacy of this final pregnancy—a diet accomplished during the months Mark had been in Rome; and he had not seen the new silhouette.

"Skin and bones," he declared in the hearty exaggerated mode they favored with each other, when they were not using the confiding or exaggeratedly dire. She looked petite again, slim and curvy, with a small waist and large breasts. She had done what gay men discovered they could do in the seventies: demand and achieve radically improved bodies. At this same weight, after a similar diet four years before, she had been unexpectedly impregnated. The idea in the family was that this now could happen again.

"Oh, you haven't seen me!" she exclaimed, and Rose said, "Doesn't she look wonderful?" Tessa made a turn in her new outfit of a body. Mark was suddenly struck through with a throb of love, for her vulnerability, her good nature and willingness to shed one third of her body weight; for the fact that this loss had both improved and aged her a little; for the notion that the clothes she wore—too bright, too young—were not hers but her elder daughter's who, that morning, had thrust these garments forward, both of them pleased to be, after all, the same size.

"You were never prettier." He wanted to say something she could get her heart's teeth into, true praise, which she seemed really to have little of from anyone.

"Well, who's coming?" Aunt Rose asked, to start them off.

"The usual suspects," he replied. "Everyone but Lord and Lady What's-it."

"Who's that?" Rose looked up from unloading the bag of groceries. George and Claudia. "Well, they never come. What's the big surprise?" She looked at him. "All you can do is ask, right?" Rhetorical questions posed in a slightly louder than normal voice, a habit they had learned, it seemed, from Margaret; the increased volume indicating unlikelihood, or irony. Rose looked at him again, closely, one eye to the other, and smiled. This meant she knew what he was doing, that he wanted the whole family there; but that this had never been easy to accomplish. She turned back to the littered countertop. "So. We're in the pink room then." She rinsed her hands and dried them thoroughly.

"Neil's coming tomorrow morning, early," Tessa said with slight defensiveness, the deserted wife. "He's climbing today." Her husband had chosen hobbies and leisure sports designed to the exclusion of the overweight: mountain climbing, bicycling, long-distance running: events in which her breasts greatly interfered; a compensatory attitude on his part, but not intentional. Whenever her slim-self stepped out of her fat-self, he understood and sympathized with more of her conversation and feelings. These slimmings and fattenings had occurred cyclically, and corresponded to the major events of their lives. It seemed, when some awful thing happened, she lost weight. And in the meantime Neil was loyal enough to stay.

While they were settling in, Mark and Bill went up to the tower, whose height and spindle railing now evoked Enzo's terrace in Rome; though Mark thought only he saw or felt the similarities, not so much in size or configuration (this was square, in Rome trapezoidal) but in their sense of commanding oceans—here of dunes, sea, sky; there of orange tiles, domes, peaks, angles, the amber ocean of Rome itself. And there was too, in both, the feeling of being close up under the sky, as if upon a platform or acropolis whose sides dropped steeply to lesser, indefensible things, lesser places; as if, this was it, as if with this small increase in height was gained a disproportionate sense of place, even of holiness—if not holiness then suitability to something special, like tea with a high lama—something in the sweep and grandeur of the placid sea and sky, or in the sudden, seldom-seen entirety of Rome perceived all at once, in both place and time; fragments made whole for the astonished eye.

"Can you hear it?" Mark asked after a moment, indicating sounds below and around them. Bill listened, dubiously; he shrugged. "I hear the ocean and your aunt."

"That's what I mean. And Tessa going on about Mara's lunch . . . The sounds coming through the rooms."

They looked at each other: communication, the look said, would be nice. "Later the house will say all this back," he explained. "It remembers the words, the simple domestic acts, like closing the refrigerator or sweeping the porch. Later I hear and see these things again . . . It's the feeling," he said, trying to explain, "that even when no one is here the house is filled with people."

"I see."

"Probably not. It doesn't matter."

"But what's the difference between this and your memory?" Bill asked gently.

"It's the house's memory, not mine."

"What's the difference?"

"Well, the difference," Mark replied, "is that it will still be here when we're gone."

*   *   *

Later towards tea Vita arrived with the youngest of her four daughters and Tessa's older girl, who were the same age and best friends, and who this summer, at seventeen, would start waitress jobs at one of the Victorian hotels. Vita herself had once done this, as had Claudia thirty years ago; the mythology of it had not changed. They would work until after lunch, then sit glorious and nubile in the sun for the rest of the afternoon: freedom came with this regimen, and they were here today with their mothers not to see Uncle Mark so much as to taste the coming summer.

Vita hugged him, gave him a look. Meeting Bill she smiled as if to say that this was the single thing she had wanted for Mark; a mate. It was in fact what she would have liked for herself. When she and Mark were alone she stepped in beside him, in her absolute direct way, touching his arm and looking up and under as if beneath the brim of a hat. "How do you feel?" she asked, meaning a clinical report of symptoms was wanted as they related to both body and mind, mood and fears. She encouraged a statement on all of this, which Mark gave, including the idea of the imagined but so far unproved effect of the Russian Cloud, the faded lesion on his heel. "The important thing," she said, "is that you think it might have happened, that it helped rather than hurt.

"—Bill seems nice," she went on. "Is there something special there?"

"The *L* word," he said simply.

"The *L* word . . ." she repeated, a look of wonder suffusing her face.

*   *   *

This was the group, since George and Claudia weren't coming, and Mr Valerian, who never slept in the house, wouldn't arrive until Sunday morning; the group as it would be for the evening, as it had stood now for some years: Mark's two sisters, without mates (one divorced, the other with entirely different interests); Aunt Rose, widowed, older, and potentially cast in the role of surrogate mother, successor to Margaret, which role she studiously, even aggressively avoided. For it was clear that while sons might occasionally like surrogate mothers, daughters usually did not, certainly not Vita or Tessa, whose mother's death, however sad, they both saw now as a liberating event. —And Mark, who until now, and like Vita, had left all possible mates at home.

In the way that a hostess will give a party with the thought of determining who her friends are, so Mark, in the dead of winter some time after Margaret's death, had invited everyone to Cape May for the weekend, it being whoever's right, when in residence, to invite the others or not. Only the girls and Rose had come. And in this way the double axis of the family had been revealed and delineated: the two Georges, and Claudia of course, who did not come; and them—the May I? Club—so named for a card game they played habitually, as they did everything habitually on those first winter nights and in the years thereafter, whenever they found themselves together; weekends repeated in each season except summer. It was not known why George and Claudia never came, always said no, with excuses; though surmise was easy and practically endless: George had said on a number of occasions that he was not really wanted; and whether this was true or not, it was the way he felt. He kept a large boat nearby; if he could get away for the day he preferred to go fishing. Coincidentally his wife's aged parents, the Kellys, had retired some years ago to the next town, so that for her Cape May was not a place of escape and idylls but the neighborhood of duty and worry, sandy guilt. George also was loathe to miss any of his young son's athletic showdowns, in successive sports, held normally on Saturdays. These were civic educational mysteries. And this particular weekend their married daughter Sarah was home from New York City. While for any of the others this would have meant that they come too, Sarah had made other plans. It came down to the simplicity of the idea that Claudia would have enjoyed herself with the May I? Club, if her own daemons allowed, which they apparently couldn't—not while her parents were still in the area, and perhaps even after they had left. And George himself would have been bored, or made vulnerable by Vita's possible judgments; and guilty, or if not guilty uncomfortable missing some small aspect of little George's athletic career.

That would do. Weekends fell apart for far less. And perhaps the reason was more basic; perhaps the prospect frightened them, was fraught in a family way; did not, for whatever reason, appeal. To understand, you had to see it all and no one saw it all.

Saturday evening Mark and Bill prepared an elaborate dinner: watercress soup, asparagus, lamb with mint sauce; Tessa's cake later with ice cream during a break in the cards. Mark set the table with candles and flowers, putting himself at the head, Tessa at the foot by the kitchen door, where she always sat, though it should have been Vita, or even Rose as the oldest—each of them had a claim; with Bill on Mark's right across from Vita: a family in the abstract; somewhere between a family and a gathering of close friends, in which, the father and mother elements being removed, all felt relaxed and amused. Mr Valerian's arrival the next day would set the balance off. At this number, the four of them with Bill, they were an integument of the family, from which many of its seeds and much of the pulp had been removed.

They each leaned toward Bill in brief ways, as they would have anyone in a sense of welcome. The three women had questions to ask in turn, beginning with the soup, when Rose looked around and said, at the point of glow-up, just before they picked up their spoons, "Mark honey, you have such a way of making things nice; you always did . . ." and looked across at Bill. "Are you a designer too, William?" She had learned that young people liked being called by their full name.

"I was. The past few years I've been caring for a sick friend. He died recently."

"I'm very sorry," Rose said and Tessa said yes.

"But I'm going back to it now." He tried to get up on a lighter note.

"Designer of what sort of thing?" Vita picked up her spoon with the cue.

"For the theatre. I do theatrical effects, sets and lighting; and magic . . . I'm interested also in magic. I want to combine the two things."

"Magic!" Rose exclaimed. "Real magic, or magic tricks?"

Bill looked across the table and considered the distinction. "Tricks that look real, that could be real someday, some way. I do spectacles that are enhanced by magic."

"How are these things produced?" Vita asked.

"In theatres, on a stage, or in some particular space— like a loft. Or in the street. I'm thinking now of a video. It's the logical extension of *tableaux vivants*."

Tessa felt compelled. "What's a tabeau . . . ?"

"It means a living picture. A posed portrait, with or without a camera. The actors depict a special moment." He looked around. "This is a tableau, of the family at home." They looked at themselves for what amounted to a performance.

"And the magic?" Vita asked.

"Well that could be just in the lighting, or something else that is emphasized—like hundreds of seed lights on threads hanging down around us over the table, or the table itself raised slightly off the ground, or the candles turning into something else . . ." he paused. "I would choose a situation that was magical to me in the first place."

Rose looked across the table with remnant tears in her eyes, smiling tears; in her case a very beautiful expression. Her husband had died one year before Margaret's illness, but had been buried three years after her death, after the dreamless tube of four years in a coma. When something moved her, Rose thought instantly of him, and sometimes the combination misted her eyes. She put her napkin to her lips. Then Mark's eyes filled too, and Bill, not quite comprehending, took Mark's hand across the corner of the table. And Tessa wiped her eyes and Vita rolled hers and said Really, and Rose fell out laughing, since somehow she was from Louisiana and knew how; but through which tearful laughter she continued to watch Bill.

Those who had not cooked then cleared and cleaned up. The dining-room chandelier was turned on to blast the bare table with light—Rose did that and Mark always dimmed it, putting out the playing cards and a cracked ugly china cup they used for the kitty. The crack made it hum. "I'm not sitting downstream of Aunt Rose," Mark declared. She usually won, her discards were worthless. Bill knew something of the game from a variation called Onze and they started right in. The first two hands went by quickly, being easy tricks, with no comment when it became clear that the last shuffle had been insufficient, in which case the table was blanketed in smug palpable silence and the quick feathery sound of cards being arranged. Rose, who knew how to play cards, began a case for her filthy luck, using terms she would never have addressed to another human being, or even to herself; to a pet perhaps. Complaining right up to the point she quietly laid down her hand, triumph compounded by surprise. During the third hand Tessa threw out the following remark with a discarded six of interest to no one: "Well, Mrs Delbono's husband died, did you hear?"

Though none of the Valerians present had met the lady, this was of the heaviest family dish. Intrigued, they all looked up; and Bill, who might have felt either at a loss, or pleased to be treated with such immediate trust to family gossip, looked politely inquisitive.

Tessa regarded her brother knowingly down the table. She'd been saving this all day, specifically for the moment between the two threes and the three and the four. Except for subject matter she'd have smiled. "Heart attack on Thursday," she added, the way you would include the batteries. "Fifty-five years old and never a day sick."

Rose had stopped, holding up a card like the wax lady in the booth, looking at Tessa over her glasses. "Who the hell is Mrs Delbono?" She threw down the card.

Which Vita took up and said, "She works at Marval."

"She's Dad's *secretary*." Tessa was vehemently specific.

"And . . ." Mark added so that the three women looked at him, while Bill took another card, half listening. ". . . She's Dad's girlfriend."

Vita, whom Mark was closely watching—since they all so valued surprising each other—widened her eyes. "She is potentially your stepmother," he said to her.

"Oh Mark, come on," Aunt Rose exclaimed, looking over his head then into his eyes with a broadening smile. "You've got to be kidding!"

"No, no!" Tessa shouted, exhilarated as always when she and her brother raced on ahead of the others. "The Delbonos were separated *five years ago*." She carefully underlined the words.

"And . . ." Mark said again and stopped.

"And what? . . . Whose turn is it?" Rose asked.

Tessa lurched and picked up a card from the pile. Rose looked at Mark. "Mark!" They all laughed. "This is excruciating! If you know something, spill it!"

Tessa discarded and they all said, May I? at once, each of them needing the card beyond desperation.

"Oh my God!" Rose exclaimed when Vita took it. "This is terrible . . . I don't have shinola."

They settled down. Mark picked up another card, appeared to be considering. Rose reached over and cuffed his shoulder.

"Well," he said, "two years ago someone selling real estate called here looking for Dad. He said a piece of land on the Allegheny had come up, adjacent to Mrs Delbono's place, and was I interested?"

"He was calling your father?" Rose said. The cards were forgotten.

"I said, Oh you mean the house on the Allegheny, and he said, Yes, Mrs Delbono's house, or rather the one in her name. I said he wasn't here and to try him at home . . . I didn't know what it meant, until now . . ."

"Holy shit," Vita said quietly. And the three of them suddenly pictured on the table the odd centerpiece of Mr Valerian embracing his secretary.

"Your father?" Rose said, incredulous.

Tessa sat with her shoulders high and her hands covering her mouth. Her gambit had developed beyond her own hopes. "Then there are all those trips," she said wonderingly. They turned back to her—the topic was again hers—a moment she used to stop, listen at the intercom on the sideboard, and say she thought she heard Mara.

"—But remember," she went on, "Remember the Hawaii trip? I called my friend Joyce in the airlines to get Dad's arrival time and she said the computer had him down into San Francisco with Mrs J D Bono."

And Vita said, ". . . And all those pictures of him in China. Andrea said who the hell is running after Pop taking all these pictures?"

"Well, I'll be damned," Rose concluded, and no one had any idea whose turn it was. "Well, you've got to hand it to him," Rose said after a moment. "It's three years later."

"A secret life," Mark observed to Vita.

"What does she look like?" Rose asked. "Does anyone know?"

"I've seen her. She's nice looking. Short, small; like Mom." Tessa blushed.

"Really, Tess."

"She's got sandy hair and wears a twelve."

Rose said, "Your mother wore a ten."

"Yes, but she's built like Mom," Tessa insisted.

"Why is he still keeping her a secret?" Mark asked, knowing why, but it was now the stage for questions.

"Well, the woman's married," Rose suggested.

"Separated," Tessa corrected, again.

"No," Vita said. "That's not it. It's Mom's image. Because of us. Pop thinks we wouldn't accept her, since he's made a saint out of Mom . . . May I?"

"Your mother *was* a saint," Rose said and gave her the card.

Mark smiled at his aunt, in perfect agreement. ". . . To put up with all of that," he said.

"You bet," Rose agreed.

"But really," Vita went on. "I mean, still not sleeping here three years later, when he's got a woman in her own house somewhere. . . . It's bizarre."

"Well, I got my toll money," Rose observed jubilantly, dropping the change she'd won into her purse. Mark and Bill were yawning. It was two hours later than they'd been up since Venice. Rose turned on the dishwasher and they all went up to bed.

In the morning, looking at Mark, Tessa asked her father how Mr Delbono's funeral had gone.

"Oh fine," Mr Valerian replied immediately, then looked up. "How'd you know about that?"

"Neil told me," she said, as if to add "of course." She knew her father would volunteer nothing on his own, so she asked how Mrs Delbono was feeling.

"Just fine," he replied warily. Sensing scrutiny, he straightened, and cleared his throat. "It was a shock, you know. Quite sudden."

"Do you think we should send a card?" Mark asked. "In which case maybe you could give us her address." Tessa blushed at the obviousness of this assault.

"I don't think that's necessary," Mr Valerian replied with a sigh, the sort of thing a large dog would say to a small cat. "She's got plenty of people around her."

Bill came down and was introduced. Mr Valerian shook his hand, having no idea who he was or why he was there. A friend of Mark's could mean anything. They sat on the porch for coffee and biscuits that Tessa had made early. Mr Valerian had brought the Sunday papers. Neil arrived and went jogging.

"George said he would stop in later, after they fish." Mr Valerian announced this casually, having been asked to do so. Like a high-wire act whose leader unexpectedly calls out the most difficult trick in the repertoire—a quadruple—they all, Vita, Tessa, Mark, and Rose, checked in with a look. Oblivious, Bill read the papers.

"George is coming here?" Vita said, her bare feet up

on the porch rail. "Have we discovered oil in the basement?"

"I suggest you all make an effort," Mr Valerian said, "since he's taking the trouble to stop."

"Trouble?" Vita said. "If it's trouble he shouldn't bother—us or himself."

"Well, you know what I mean . . . Please, Vita," he said wearily. She put her feet down and shaded her eyes, looking out to sea.

"And Claudia?" Tessa took it up. "Is she coming too?"

"I think they're all coming," he replied. "Sarah and the baby, Abby and little George . . ."

"Ye Gods," Tessa exclaimed. "Are all these people going to want to eat? She told me she wasn't coming . . ."

"Well I understand Sarah thought it was a good idea," Mr Valerian said.

"But you know," Rose put in, "Claudia never arrives anywhere without all the fixin's."

In fact Claudia arrived some time later with her older daughter Sarah and six-month-old grandson, stopping at the front door to admire the garden. An impulsive March morning at the nursery and a warm, wet spring had given the front border unexpected style. They all now embraced amid the blooms. Centrally radiant, as if lighted from within by his own whiteness, Sarah's baby glowed, fuzzily, in perfect infancy. Sarah held him this way and that, as you do a mirror to the sun, tilting the light in their eyes to dazzle them. The baby was big, looking ten or twelve months old rather than six, frowning back at them with wise collected

concern that suddenly dissolved into a delighted gur-
gling smile, flashing in turn the momentary faces of
both his parents. Mark and Bill approached but did not
touch. Anyway Rose took the baby in her arms and
they all went into the house. Rose's own daughter had
a baby girl a few months older, and as she held Sarah's
child in her arms, Rose hefted the difference. This one,
though younger, was heavier, like good silver. His fat-
ness of health, the white *velouté royale* skin glowed
indoors, like Madame Curie's purse in her darkened
lab. Rose forgot comparisons, which she knew to be
odious, and tried to duplicate the baby's incredible
lightness of expression: the lifting of the eyes, eyebrows, even hairline, a curving upward of everything, a
levitation of being. Rose did her best.

"Mark, do you want to hold him?" Sarah asked,
looking up with her baby's grown face and startling
Mark out of his wits. Beside them Claudia seemed to
flinch but not actually move. It had seemed remote that
Sarah would ask. They had discussed it.

"I'd better not come too close," he said.

"Why not?"

"Someone was here with the flu this week and I feel
a little throaty." He thought this was adequate, but
apparently not. Meanwhile Claudia took the baby and
hoisted him up face to face, asking unanswerable loving questions as a diversion.

Then George appeared, having called earlier from his
boat to say they had hit something and would be
delayed; sunburned in odd, unselfconscious patterns
and smelling faintly of the fish they had caught. These
went into the freezer beside a collection of past catches

that no one would eat, for the mercury, but which George continued to bring home. Considering the cost of his fishing expeditions, involving a half-million-dollar, sixty-foot fishing yacht with captain and mate, fuel and insurance—the fish going into the freezer (where their chances for revival equaled those of Walt Disney in Anaheim) were worth something like six hundred dollars apiece. Though you could not put a price on the relaxation, the sense of calm, George would have said.

Except that Mark had kept more hair, they were very alike physically. George shorter. Also their voices, especially on the telephone, and even to Claudia and his secretaries, were indistinguishable. As they got older they had seemed to look more alike; this was true of all four of them. His two sisters each day sleepily glimpsed their mother's face in the morning mirror, as if bumping into her on the landing—older, dishevelled, bleary with sleep, then gone for the day. Of the four, perhaps Mark seemed most like Margaret, they would have said, because of the eyes. Though George's eyes were the same shape and color he did not have the look, nor would he have wanted it, which he characterized as anxious, needful, sad. In fact he resented it. Mr Valerian, if he had noticed anything beside the new absence of defiance, had long since repressed the similarity.

George III, now twelve, had come with his father; they spent all weekends together as part of the formula, ironclad and not to be broken. Young George was blond, favoring his mother's side rather than the Valerians, intelligent, considerate, pubescent, agile, healthy. George could not look at or talk to him without an exaggeration of expression or tone, in voice or eyes.

The last vestiges of George's body's youth and suppleness were devoted to the continuing education of this youngster. He was all. Barely a teenager, he could beat his father at everything now but chess. Culturally, he was too old to kiss his uncle, but usually did, or hugged him; so that now Mark dropped back and cuffed him affectionately instead. Only Tessa's children called Mark Uncle, and they only because Tessa had vetoed his request that they not. In the same sentence Sarah would say, Aunt Tessa and Mark, or Mark and Aunt Vita, as if each time his request for equality devolved again, making them contemporaries, or cousins and friends as they were among themselves. Had it been for them or for him, this informality? to add to their position, or to make him seem younger? He was their intermediary, lingering between the generations; who, if they wished—they had only to ask—would act as their guide through the emotional muck. He had done it often, especially for Sarah, since she was the oldest and first of that generation, and in many ways the one who earliest and best understood the differences in Mark. None of these differences had surprised her, though it seemed her generation, or her part of it, was easily shocked. In the way he had not wanted them to address him as Uncle, he did not want them to know he was ill.

Presently he and George found themselves alone, sitting in the angle of the low chevron wall overlooking the beach, on what might have been called the East Lawn. Mark had names for everything. This was the Bow. A circle of wicker chairs at one end of the porch was the Geneva Convention. At the other end, the gazebo end, was Captain Bird's Bridge. Christina's World constituted a spit of lawn on the north side where it dipped down and raised the house against a ravening sky. Vita's second daughter, Andrea, an artist, had one day spent most of the afternoon as the girl in the painting, framed, for the benefit of those passing by.

It was the moment before lunch, not a good time to start anything; Vita was nearby on the porch reading while the others, including Mr Valerian, who lately had taken an interest in the preparation of food, were in seeing about the contents of the baskets Claudia had brought.

"Listen," his brother said quietly, leaning forward to prevent Vita from overhearing. "While we have a moment . . . and I hope you'll take this the way it's intended, as something that must be dealt with . . . And by the way, how are you feeling?" Here you had George, or a lot of him. In this speech could be found the springs of his conflict: self-interest and compassion in unequal parts—interest in something that apparently would upset Mark when he heard it; and compassion, also for Mark who, after all, was his brother, a part of himself.

"I feel fine," Mark replied, "other than fatigue in the afternoon and headaches."

"And Bill?" George asked.

Mark hesitated.

"I assume he's gay."

"Yes, as a matter of fact."

"Is he okay?"

The question meant was Bill sick. "Why do you ask?"

"Because he's gay, Mark. It's a natural question."

"Meaning logical?" Mark heard or felt something tip, a slippage of delicate machinery, or perhaps of gold chains in the palm of the hand, a faint metallic sound. He leaned forward and asked what it was George wanted to say.

"Well, it's the same thing," George replied in a voice he sometimes used with juries—a number-nine iron in the rough—a tone of bewilderment, of sudden confusion. He was good with his voice, unselfconscious and versatile. They all were, with a command of quick, ironic, even sarcastic directness, not always humorous, but often humorous. "If Bill is also ill . . ." He stopped as Vita came over.

She had not been listening, or more exactly, had not heard it all, but had caught this last part. George might now have asked her to stay out of it, but he might also have brought up the subject because Vita was within range.

So George looked up. "It's Sarah's—it's my daughter's right to know, *to protect her baby.*" He spoke in legal italics. Vita sat down beside Mark. "Bill's got it, too," George added.

"So I understand," Vita replied. "I'm sorry . . . But I don't see how that affects you or Sarah."

"If you had a newborn baby, you would want to know that two people in the house have a dangerous disease that no one understands."

Vita and Mark regarded him. ". . . And you would want to have the choice to stay or leave," he concluded. "It's as simple as that."

"It's even simpler, George." Vita stood up. "Why don't you mind your own fucking business?"

"Sound psychological advice," he said dryly.

"You wouldn't know sound psychological advice if it crawled up your nose . . . You have the sensitivity and compassion of a fishhook," she went on in a quiet voice. "Don't you think there's enough trouble here without your adding to it? The fact is, George, there *is* no danger. It's just for today. Besides, they haven't touched the baby, so dry up." She went into the house.

Later when Mark was coming up the stairs Sarah was putting the baby down in the pink room. The pink room off the landing was where the crib lived. Sarah looked up and smiled; the baby against her shoulder was too excited to sleep; and since they were always together they now played quietly. Sarah had stripped him to diapers, fitting, Mark noticed, like the hand-embroidered pantaloons of the *Enfantina*. The baby's skin, into which, like the finest white pâté, unto mousse, the flesh was forced, was a matte, sheer, translucent glaze. How obvious to all who did not themselves have babies that cannibalism, as an instinct, was as old nearly as hunger itself; the root of the biblical threat, to families, of unattached males: that they will eat your young; that in a world in extremis, babies have often been considered succulent delectables, to be guarded in gilded food safes—their cribs—and suspended in alcoves of taboo. Mark and Sarah sat on the end of the bed as the baby—beyond good-natured, into benevolence—stood up against the railing of the crib as at the balcony of a tall palace or cathedral, and blessed his mother, his great-uncle Mark, with fake smiles of immense beauty. They watched his expressions evolve and shift, alter and fade, a time-stop picture of his own glee like a flower opening and closing; until with a bump he lost his grip, hit his lip, and looked up at his mother, all in an instant, in sudden wonder, sudden doubt. In the same instant Sarah felt Mark flinch and said quietly, "Don't react," and Mark watched his niece, whom he could vividly recall holding at this age, smile brightly at her baby, unperturbed, unaffected, untouched by any possible harm to the two perfect little teeth or lips. Nasty black bird fly over. Not so much recovering as making an ironic comment, already a student of the ironic, the baby returned the smile, and at whom they roared as if at Jack Benny's best joke.

"You have just saved this child endless lonely nights and hours of computer dating," Mark observed.

"Oh Mark!" Sarah laughed. Even the baby laughed.

"Who taught you that?" he asked her. "Tessa would have done her Maria Callas imitation for less."

Claudia came in. "She certainly didn't learn it from me."

The large house was filled now with people moving about. Tessa's son had come to get a surfboard out of the garage. The two middle girls, Tessa's and Vita's, were downstairs beside the toaster, each on one leg like graceful birds, discussing in the driest terms a woman on the beach with enormous cracked emeralds. George and Mr Valerian, in Geneva, were talking business in stupefying detail, to which Neil listened with the attention of a boy by the window enthralled with the view. To him, as to all the Valerian in-laws, this on its own was paradise. Tessa and Rose, in the kitchen, cooked. Vita and Bill had gone for a walk around the pond. Most of the children, including the mother's helper and Mara, were on the beach.

With Claudia now, Sarah and Mark watched the baby—a sensation not unlike watching TV—who was at last settling down. Claudia and Sarah had been earlier to the Kelly house to present this fourth or fifth great-grandson. Most of Claudia had returned; not all. In a moment she would go back for the rest. Her parents were old, too old sometimes to be nice to each other even in the act of being nice enough to live on indefinitely. They were waiting. Claudia looked at Mark when she said she had to go back, and Mark thought, but did not say, I know everything about your life, and you know all about mine, and still I love you, love you for it, and hope you love me. But he said, "I know how difficult it must be." And Claudia wanted to say it was a curse to live so long, but could not, given the circumstances. It seemed she never liked to disappoint him by saying the obvious, and often, as a result, said startling things. She and Mark did know a great deal about each other, it had been so long, but they had not understood something basic until later: that in the newspaper personals of his mind Mark had long since placed a running ad for Sisters—it was as sisters that he best understood women, indeed people; until now they had been the easiest relationships of his life. But Claudia had five brothers, and Mark's familiarity in this regard was to her a kind of threat. Of intimacy perhaps; she may have felt that five brothers were enough. Nor was she particularly close either to Vita or Tessa, both of whom—had Claudia herself been in the market for sisters—would willingly have committed. It may have seemed to her, because of five people and their broods who waited in the wings, for a production that would not end but *begin* with the imminent deaths of their aged parents, that a choice loomed—between the Kellys and the Valerians: a question of style, of pace; and that essentially Claudia preferred the Kellys and her natural position among them to the Valerians, whose vacant matriarchal throne, she noticed, no one seemed eager to occupy.

Before dinner Mark presented himself in Geneva, from which Mr Valerian in good weather seldom stirred. When it was just them his father said, "I understand you're about to choose a drug." Mark had mentioned this to Tessa, or perhaps to Vita.

"Dr Thompson thinks there's something in this new treatment," he said, and named an antiviral in the news. All the drugs had letters for names; it was clear only that when he did choose, it would be from an alphabet soup. Mark named a famous person who for some months, through sheer personal influence and presumably unlimited funds, had obtained this drug before anyone else.

"Must you choose?" his father asked. "Aren't you feeling more or less the same?"

He was not. The naps were now half the afternoon, headaches every morning. There was a lump under the skin just below the sternum, like a disk, that had appeared in the last few days. "Who knows what's going on inside," he said vaguely. Mr Valerian peered over as if surmising the deterioration; as if he might see for himself. 'Yes,' the look said. He too, at seventy-five, thought vaguely of inside. "Yes, well," he said finally, "you shouldn't be too quick with your eggs." Abbreviation gave force to cliché, a family habit.

"Bill's got it, too," Mark said abruptly.

"I know. Your brother told me."

"I thought he might."

"You can't blame him, Mark. A man worries about his children. It's only natural."

"Is it unnatural to worry a little about your brother?"

Raised eyebrows meant yes, of course, but so what? "What are your plans?"

"Bill has inherited a place in western Mass. We'll go up there for a while . . . Perhaps stay until Dr Thompson says it's time to start." Out to sea the light was fading; the color of the water was merging with the sky, everything the same blue. Inside, one of the girls who took French in the tenth grade announced, *"L'heure bleu!"* Aunt Rose said, "What's that, honey?" The porch door opened and Tessa said Dinner in twenty minutes.

Mark's reactions to being what others called fatally ill—you could be fatally, mortally, or terminally ill: they were not the same—were similar to having been through his mother's demise. It was something that had happened, to which he had variable responses occurring in gradual stages, and not simply a state of on-going panic, fear, grief. It felt now, since panic had left him, that he would survive (panic itself following on the certainty of doom), or perhaps the absence of panic was itself a stage, akin to fear, and fear alone in comparison was not so bad. He thought many times, What do you do, other than be afraid? With the passage of time, with the arrival of Bill, it seemed even fear had abated, if not disappeared. It was not something he thought about often. Death itself, apparently, had retreated, again becoming the abstract notion it was to most people—not real, not imminent; dying perhaps, but not death.

These were fine distinctions. Death was a fine distinction, while life remained a gross abundance of everything—of waste, plenty, squandered time—in the sheer inability to accommodate all it offered and contained: air not breathed, billions of people, places to be, ways of being, thought itself; a horror of waste. Even death now, like life, appeared to be a matter of opinion. Some thought you never died, but changed into something else, somewhere else; went to another dimension. For instance, his mother in Rome. She was dead but appeared often in dreams, like a dead film star on late-night TV movies. Even now, if he asked them, Vita, Tessa and George would willingly recount their dreams of Margaret, evidence of a continuing connection. Vita would now say she equated these dreams with the need to move on, to be rid of all of it; George—that Margaret frequently reminded him to throw the garbage (meaning, Vita would point out, that George felt guilty for shirking imagined responsibilities—the failure of the Marval deal perhaps). And Tessa's dreams, rather like Mark's, involved specific situations—for Tessa often a children's playground or the beach—for him an apartment in Rome or a train station. This he thought was a kind of immortality; or, if not, then at least vitality after the fact. In their dreams Margaret was still being mother, efficiently filling the cup (pouring out the tea) of need.

What had not abated was the feeling of being cheated,

as an innocent party, out of half his time as Mark Valerian. People so casually cleared eighty these days, staying on until they resembled nothing so much as some dazed decrepit thing waiting for a train.

☆

Leaving the car in the woods on the other side of the lake, they used a canoe for the last leg of the trip, though the road led directly to a driveway behind the lodge. But canoeing was the equivalent of Bill's having sent a limo to the airport: the best approach to the situation. The slender lake was long and riverine, each end curved away and disappeared in the trees. Gliding across, Mark could see nothing on the other side, then low on the edge a weathered dock that sipped the water, and a faded lawn chair in a clearing beyond; as they drew nearer, a second chair. The water had stilled to glass, the lake was tipped up toward them like a mirror on the wall. Then thirty feet away the pieces of a big gray shape, its outline broken and scattered, neatly assembled itself, a solid mass amid the lacy boughs, leaves, and black trunks. And he thought how romantic and private, sheltered and odd it looked. No birds, or sounds. They disembarked. Neither spoke but looked at the other every few seconds, Bill's calm matching Mark's wonder. From the dock the camp stood up on moss and blooming laurel so overgrown as to look treelike. Nothing had been cut back in years, except that saplings reached for a space in the canopy left by a felled oak, fifty years old, which lay to rot along the ground and into the brush. A green room growing in on itself, left to its own fecund devices; something of the temple reclaimed by jungle, of the southern river palace gone to seed. It was properly a house, three storeys high, but built along the lines of a summer cabin, a camp, a lodge; all of wood, with a big screened-in porch across the front. From which, beyond the taller trees as through the fingers of his hands, the ribbon of lake ran by.

Bill had mentioned a sense of abandonment, and had not been back in two years. The door was padlocked, windows shuttered. An arrangement had long ago been made with a local man to empty the pipes in fall and prime them in spring, but apart from this it was not the sort of place you kept up with. Beyond the laurel it had no garden and had never been painted, its gray color being the weathered hardness of whatever wood had gone into it. The roof was mossy tin. Outer walls stopped eighteen inches below the eaves, beneath which ran screened strips for ventilation in summer, again like a cabin, with wooden flaps on hinges to be put up in a storm or other seasons. A house meant to live on its own, meant to freeze over and sleep in winter and to thaw and dry out in spring like the trees themselves.

It had been Fred's, who as a child had helped his father and uncles to build it. Now all had died. Its secrets and half its history were gone. What was known stood here, fifty years later, unchanged but for the plumbing, added later. Not water you would want to drink, since it came from the lake; plus the earth box still standing at the end of a pine-needle path. Cleverness with ventilation, drainage, the lay of the land, playing the sun through the trees like a sundial—secrets now lost. Fred's parcel ran all the way around the lake. Fishermen had used a clearing at the west end as a ramp until Fred planted and sealed it off for privacy. But sometimes still the locals took boats out somehow and like people who, by fief, may sit or keep their hats on in the Queen's presence, went for pickerel and trout.

Now, through the trees, not much of the lake was visible from the porch. Eventually Bill and Mark pruned enough for more of a view, like the slit in a bunker; and each day swept more of the lodge, cleaned the windows, removed spider webs which next morning were replaced in the same spots, until these were left to display the currents and delicacies of spider life. Outside, where there might have been bare earth, were moss and lichens; where there might have been weeds were ferns and mushrooms and a flower like a white buttercup. Where there might have been trees, the laurel, usually low to the ground, was after some wild years now eight and ten feet tall. The trees themselves, chosen and spared as deliberately as columns fifty years earlier, loomed over the lodge like servants with wraps and umbrellas. In between—something he had not seen at first—the trunks of slender white birches stood out like ribs amid the dark verdigris of pine and fir. Shaded over by the canopy the space around the house seemed contained and separate, a space cubed to the height of the trees in which birds swam languidly from limb to limb like fish, hovering in the air, the refracted light striking everything an endless deepening lightening green.

Inside, a wood stove dried the air, warmed the belly of the lodge which by ten popped as he walked through;

not the fire in the stove, which had gone out, but the wood of the house itself, dried in and out, creaking joins and joints making small sudden cries. Up beneath the intricate roof was a single open room in which the rain on the tin rattled and snared like a drum. Here they removed all but one bed, table, and bureau, and napped each afternoon as in the translucent coil of a shell burnished by light at one end. Lying in bed like falling over a waterfall clutched together head to toe, they slept and half awakened to make love in the racket. At night they woke each other from bad dreams as if saving each other's lives—from vivid dreams whose themes of danger, separation and hopelessness sounded in small desolate cries. "It's all right," the other said, would say. "It's just a dream," since dreams meant nothing; as if simply to be told it wasn't real was enough.

Each day held four kinds of weather: cold; then cool saturated verdant spring; heat at noon, leading to short ferocious summer rains, and ending in a comfortable autumn twilight. The rooms as they dried smelled of camphor and clover or hay. The furniture made locally for the house was flat planes of maple, with chintz cushions. No electricity, they used oil lamps and candles in the pitch-dark nights, the only time they heard anything outside: rustling leaves, cracked twigs, frogs, a night owl across the lake whose call according to local parlance, Bill said, was 'Come for the ale, not for the beer.' From the dock the hilly ring of trees encircling the lake became an inverted bowl of stars that multiplied before their eyes; holding hands, silent to hear the lake, the brightest stars appeared, with smaller, dimmer, distant points glimmering a million at a time.

Evenings, when its surface went flat and a pair of efficient kingfishers worked the lake, they went out in the canoe, each time to a different quadrant. At the east end a small marsh was crammed with lily pads and grasses that whispered and hugged the canoe. Here, in profile, a stately heron waited when they came near, and it seemed the silence of the marsh emanated from this blue fire. The west end poured itself slowly over an eight-foot sluice into a web of brown-colored brooks. All around, rising slopes of forest moved up the hill, giving the lake the shape and acoustics of a great amphitheater, and at dusk the least sound carried from one side to the other. When Mark went canoeing alone he was able from far out in the middle to talk quietly with Bill on the dock. This phenomenon perhaps seemed in a way an extension of what happened inside the lodge where, with the thin wood walls and rooms stacked one on the other, each murmur was overheard, upstairs or down—an alternative conversation of asides and commentary that quickly became habitual. All people who live alone talk to themselves, and it thrilled Mark the first few times it happened, that on remarking to himself how quiet or beautiful it all was, Bill answered him.

The connection between them had grown in a matter of weeks—scarcely a month—to an exhausting need, manifested in constant contact. This would have presented a physical problem had their fatigue, their malaise, been less evenly matched. But a balance was struck between what they would have liked and required from each other's bodies and what they each could give. To hold, to be held, seemed a great deal; to behold, to hold hands, to be together; the slow intense passion of the elderly. They were sick in similar ways: brief headaches, a propensity for depression and sleep that was inverse and predictable; good appetites but occasional nausea; maturing lesions that slowly thickened but did not hurt. None of it was worse than what you might feel on the last days of flu. The physical side seemed balanced, in their case, by the absence of what might have made it worse: loneliness, the fear of doing this alone, whatever it was or would be—a gradual decline, in imperceptible stages. They were not afraid simultaneously; it seemed one's fear stimulated the other to protectiveness. Fear was the dream they woke each other from.

Fred had said, Don't go to the lake until afterwards, and could not be persuaded while he was ill to visit even for a weekend. But later he had told Bill to drop his ashes in the middle. This, after some time now, Bill had not yet done, although at last he was here with the bottle. He showed it to Mark. "It's Fred," he said. "He wanted to be scattered on the lake."

Mark looked out to check conditions. The bottle was opaque white plastic with a screw top. He wondered if ashes would sink. Bill thought the hour should be dusk, when spirits hung over the surface asleep and then quietly wakening; not at dawn, since dawn was cold and unreceptive, the morning mist on the lake being the gas remnant of a medium inhabited for the night, and which at sunrise, in wisps, burned off like steam.

After their nap they got in the canoe and glided out to the middle, for a while drifting and watching the stillness. On the bank the forest was picked out in realistic crewelwork, its reflection below repeated out of focus in bargello. Bill said, "Fred thought his family were all out here, waiting for him. Whenever we were here at this hour he would sit on the dock or come out and float around." Bill screwed the top off the bottle and tipped some of the ashes onto the glassy water, where they lay on the surface without sinking. He stirred them a little with his finger. He turned in the seat and looked back at Mark.

They watched the floating debris. After a while three small pickerel arrived and poked speculatively from below. Some of it went down, not all. Bill sifted out a bit more, then more, a little at a time. They drifted and waited. Regrettably the ashes looked like vomit. "Would you say this is going to work, or not?" Bill asked in a whisper. The trail of ashes lay in an irregular spiral, widening slightly on the imperceptible current. Mark said it might be better to dump it all at once. Bill turned the bottle upside down and Fred's remains fell straight through the surface of the lake as if diving from the bottle. Below, in a kind of powdery eruption, the ashes were liquefied. He shook the bottle and scattered more dusty remnants like feathers on the surface, like powder on a mirror. The point was that you could wind up as ashes on a lake. Bill said, "I'm going to talk a little about Fred." He looked around the lake. Mark looked out at the same thing, the wet paddle across his knees.

"We met in a bar. He asked me to come home with

him . . . Fred never announced what he was going to do. He just did it and showed you. He showed me he loved me. He sent me to school, got me work with his friends. Did everything. He loved me and I loved him. He was the sweetest, gentlest man I ever knew. He said his people were here waiting, and that I was to do everything I could to keep this place the way it is. I will do that . . . Fred, this is Mark, whom I also love, though I didn't plan it that way. We met because we need each other . . . I don't know, because he's a little like you. Because life takes something and gives back something else . . . I hope you don't mind. I know you don't. Being alone is the worst, the last thing. I couldn't come here alone . . ." He looked back at Mark and trailed his hand in the water. "I couldn't do anything alone now."

Later they discussed this small ceremony as if it had been staged by someone else. "Some sort of quiet delicate music would have been nice," Bill said. "Fred loved Chopin." The next evening when it was again time to go canoeing Mark said, "Let's go and see Fred." Bill set his cassette player on the dock and a tape of Chopin's Etudes drifted out over the lake like wind through the chandelier. When they got back they found a large black cat sitting on the dock, apparently attracted to the source of the music, its black cutout shape the last thing to be seen in the gathering dusk. It did not run off as they docked. Mark fed it, and if staying meant reappearing for meals, it stayed. A lesser, unafraid panther, half wild, it spent mornings hunting, which meant sitting perfectly still in a certain spot behind the lodge, waiting for movement or sound. It was of course Fred, Bill said. But Mark thought it was Romolo, his clairvoyant friend from Rome; or Romolo's *familiar*. Bill observed the two black filberts between its legs. "It's been through two or three winters, at least. *Someone's* been feeding it," he said. Because of something matted in the end of the tail it appeared to be forked at the tip. The next evening at dusk, from around the corner of the lodge, the cat spoke once to announce its presence and jumped onto Mark's lap, where it lay solidly, warmly on Mark's genitals, purring as if having come for the purpose, or as if having done it before. Mark blushed and got an erection, which the cat gripped warmly through his shorts.

"This cat . . ." Mark began.

"What's it doing?"

"It seems to be getting off."

"It's purring," Bill observed.

"It feels like an acujack." Mark scratched behind the cat's ears. It didn't like this and shook its head to a blurred double. He touched the hindquarters and it lifted itself against the pressure, curving its back into a position that yogis call the scorpion, which culminates in an open sphincter, and which now was greatly enhanced by the bifurcated tail.

"A gay cat," Bill said.

At the country store/post office, the postmistress did not know of such a creature and offered to put a description on the bulletin board. However she left off *Cat* and put simply, *Black Male Found*, making it sound like a runaway slave, laughing when this was pointed out to her and ripping it down. She said the woods were full of half-wild cats. She handed them a

postcard and a letter, both for Mark, the postcard from
Tessa asking him to call; the letter from Matthew Black.

Lake Louise, June 15

Face of the Doll,

    The North woods darling; plaid shirts, wood
stoves, pine needles: a lesbian fantasyland.
Edith Wharton does Lenox. I was of course there
years ago, the mandatory North Woods romance so alluded to in the seventies, the vision
you find yourself at the center of, except that
I was not in love with the host, merely his willing love-slave. Yes Fred, though ever so briefly
and it never amounted to much, we were so polite with each other, and that only works when
one of you is considerably older—like for instance Fred and Bill. Fred was the gentleman
of an earlier age, who—had he lived— would
have become saintly. Or, to put a fine point
on it, would have come to look more like what
he always was: a holy man. While Mother, of
course, and at *such* a young age, had other things
in mind (Pardon but did you expect me to get
through tea without an erection?) It took really
just one weekend to see it wouldn't work for
us—Rita Hayworth afraid of snakes and in all
the wrong clothes, ravishing, hot and frankly
bored. I thought he needed someone less ver-
bal, in less of a hurry. Someone with whom
he could fish, by the hour, from a little boat in
the middle of the lake.

You will have realized by now the dire lack
of lake images in our culture. It begins and
ends with Walden and Golden Pond. "Boa! Boa!
Boa!" A lake is a lake, though often a pond.
Is it all you expected? It was Fred's obsession.
The difference, between that one and this, is
the privacy. The peace. Ours is more of a bay
and free-for-all; motorboats, water skiers orange in the sunset sending up cockatoo waves
that catch the light. When the wind is wrong
you can hear children having a good time, which
after a crying baby is the most irritating sound
known to man. Quiet in Florida is something
you imagine, or remember. But a lake nonetheless. We have our ducks and egrets, even our
blue heron, the Jacqueline Onassis of birds,
which spends all of its time shopping in the next
cove. When I drive by I see it indifferently pick-
ing through the bins. We have too a new kind
of algae here, half-plant, half-chemical, that
comes to the surface every day, turns everything to jelly and drags it to the bottom. It
looks like a cross between clouds and rocks, but
dirty. This is referred to as "the lake working," though I think it must have something to
do with the weapons factory whose stacks I
can see through binoculars. Imagine letting your
kids swim in it. As they do. A kind of genetic
obliviousness to the real. Ignorance. Do you
follow?

Went to Gville the other night to a bar, and
met someone—not of this world—who said to
wait for him outside. I went out and waited,

rather endlessly, trembling with fear and excitement. Could something I would do this time
give It to me? Or tip the scales? But I could not
stop myself. Finally he came out of the bar,
immediately ran into three friends, who turned
him around and took him back inside. The RE-
LIEF of not having to go through with it, the
horror of thinking I would have. The DISAP-
POINTMENT. Capitals fail. We go from living
like monks to committing acts of sexual suicide. Is this wise? What is needed is a condom
bodysuit, at least a rubber for the tongue. This
would equate with the first human tool use for
ingenuity and race genius . . .

"Fred and Matthew?" Mark said.

"Fred said he never laughed like he did with Matthew and it made him fall in love. And they had danced
together in the old days."

"In twenty years, Matthew has never mentioned him
once."

"It lasted two months, if that. Matthew thought Fred
wasn't passionate, which wasn't true. You just had to
get him started."

Tessa had just wanted to say hello and ask, in a half
voice, how it was, meaning primarily the cabin, though
she might have meant the mosquitoes, or the neighbors. Perhaps she meant all of it. It reassured Tessa to
speak in what he would call familiar terms, rather than
for instance mentioning the stillness or the mysterious
beauty of the lake. They were very well, she said, as if

the past two weeks had contained inexplicably avoided disasters.

The news was that Vita had had lunch with Neil, at her request. It seemed that George lately had been pushing again to sell the beach house.

"But we settled that," Mark said, alarmed. "They promised."

"I'm only telling you what Neil said. Maybe you'd better talk to him."

"I can't do it on the phone."

"When are you coming home?" Tessa hoped that later on, when this came out, she would not be held responsible. But Mark went back to it. "Look, Tess, are you saying . . . I mean is Neil saying that George is urging Dad to sell?"

"Well, George thinks we can't afford to pass up these offers."

On another trip to the post office he called Vita. She was, as usual, inclined to be calm, awaiting developments.

"It does seem to be worth a lot," she said.

"When I get back . . ." Mark began.

"I wouldn't rush home. It's hot as hell."

"It can wait, you think?"

"Mark, I wouldn't get involved on that level. They can't do anything without us; and I promise, Tessa and I won't agree . . . George thinks up his little schemes. But listen—remember—they are often stymied by the sheer weight of the bullshit they pile on each other's heads."

He laughed. She did not. "But I wouldn't dwell," she concluded. "It all sounds more like Neil letting the dogs loose, if you ask me."

The cat was there each morning early, and at dinnertime the sound of the can opener, or the smell of fishfinger stew brought it to the door. At dusk it sat in their laps on the dock, later waiting there as they glided across the lake in one direction or another, its eyes following them intently. As the days went by and they got better at canoeing, they appeared on the lake without sound, without a knock of the paddles or splash of water; as if stirring slowly but powerfully a huge cauldron of thick brown soup. They learned to glide, as the alligator glides, as a log on the current, half in the water; so that more of the lake was revealed. Birds and fish stayed where they were, even the heron who waited and waited for the first signs of treachery to flee. For an hour or so each evening a million spiders danced on the surface like rain, with tiny spreading circles as far as you could see. One evening in the fourth week Bill took him out to the middle as the last daylight was fading.

He had been gone most of the day and had missed his nap. Through binoculars Mark had watched him doing something along the opposite bank. "A few more minutes," he whispered.

"What?" Mark whispered back.

"You'll see." It grew darker as the sun fell farther behind the hill, the trees black; the lake alone held dull silvery light in puddles. The first stars came out, one in particular. "Now watch."

Along the bank, pockets of light had seemed refracted from the disappeared sun. Merely an effect. As it grew darker these lights got stronger, brighter, each with a small reflection bleeding into the water; a necklace of lights ran along the bank from one end to the other.

"How did you do that?"

"Magic," Bill said with a smile. ". . . A generator, lights, miles of extension cord."

"I don't hear a generator."

"It's there. In an insulated box."

The trees, lighted from beneath, delineated the graceful curve of the lake.

"Is this for me, or for Fred?"

"It's for everyone. Do you like it?"

"It's beautiful. It's amazing . . . I see eyes over there . . ." Two tiny dots of red light hovered amid the twigs and leaves at the edge, caught by the spotlights. They blinked out, came on again. "An owl maybe."

They went closer. "Is it all permanent?" Mark asked.

"Nothing's permanent. But it can be maintained."

"What would Fred think?"

"I don't know. Maybe that it's nonsense, that there's enough light during the day . . ."

From the porch the lights bleeding into the black water placed the house exactly in the darkness, as if at the edge of a busy harbor or estuary. Another time, Bill went out again and was gone until their nap. Late in the afternoon they awoke to the sound of falling water, though not sounding on the roof. A jet of water shot sixty feet into the air over the marsh at the west end. Late sun hit the spray in a wedge of rainbow carried to one side by the breeze. As they approached the jet, bright colors blazed over them, to the point of just feeling an outer mist falling off the wind like talc. The two herons and several ducks were arriving, presumably also the pickerel. Bill showed him a pipe running through the reeds to the bank.

"I added a pump," he said. "The generator can't handle both. By day it does the pump, at night the lights."

"How did you do all this alone?"

"I didn't. A plumber did the pipe. An electrician did the generator. I watched. Still . . ."

The water jet jumped high in the air, bouncing at the top and tumbling on its weight. As the sun went down, the lights came on in sudden silence. The jet had a tendency to clog. Occasionally the automatic timer didn't catch, the lights were on all day, golden in the brush.

One weekend, at their request, Vita arrived, flying like the Empress-Pope to the nearest airport, enthralled from the moment the plane landed in what seemed like a clearing in the woods. Woods were to Vita the thing, as the beach had been to Mark, recalling the neutral ground of childhood. They drove her the scenic way, through the corner of a state forest that the lake abutted, through the sad, huge trees of the Berkshires— groves of pines like Karnak, fields of willows with their skirts uniformly hemmed, ravines filled with mossy rocks. They stopped to admire a stupendous waterfall, at the beauty of which Vita lightly wept. "Vita," he said sternly, "you don't stand a chance, if you think this is anything. This is a pathetic natural occurrence . . ." The short canoe ride across the lake surprised and delighted her. Mark in the stern pushed off the rocks, turning her toward the lodge, visible now through the trees on the other side like a face at a curtain.

"Is that it?" she said breathlessly. "I think I'll wet my pants this time . . . There's nothing left to do."

The cat sat waiting on the dock, let itself be petted. "My eyeteeth," she declared, looking up at the lodge. It was four o'clock; no thought of a nap. She changed into jeans and they went out again for the water jet and light show. "Oh!" she cried involuntarily, when the jet came on, followed instantly by a reverberant crack of wings as the birds flew into the air all at once, like the lake itself leaping up, gradually falling back to what they had been doing. Later, with the lights on, Vita went out again by herself, at their urging. When she returned she was ready to talk. They had dinner on the porch, up over the lake, a shape now contained within its necklace of lights, these in addition to the reflection also of the brighter stars.

"This place is magic," she said. "Though it's difficult to tell what you've done from what was here. . . . It's not something anyone would think of," she said, looking out at the lake. "It would not occur to anyone to string electric lights around a pond in the middle of nowhere."

"Except the duchess of Devonshire at Chatsworth," Mark suggested. "You had to see it, Vita," he said, "since it all means so much."

"I don't think of them as electric lights," Bill said. "They are life forms, they are our guests. They live here by the water, and glow at night."

"Life forms," she repeated.

"From the future, in which the lake is a hotel for visitors from another planet; where everyone is an electric current. They speak the language of brightness.

— 148 —

They are not exactly electricity, but electricity does for them here, the way pure oxygen would do for us in their world."

"And the water jet?" she asked.

"The jet comes from a natural hot spring, from a different geologic past, in which the lake fills a volcanic crater beneath which lies a steam vent, now nearly cool. I wish it could start and stop all day, at random . . . as if these things had happened to the lake, you see."

"Wasn't it a lot of work?" she asked.

"I suppose it was expensive, more than anything else."

"And very Western," she added. "In the East they would leave it in pristine darkness."

"We can still do dark," Mark suggested. He looked at Bill. "I have at last found a man who understands the point of existence is the rearrangement of the furniture."

"But Mark," Vita said, and stopped. ". . . For you, maybe. Some people prefer disorder. Or don't notice it."

"Nobody we know," Bill said.

At another point, and perhaps referring to the impulse behind the lights and water jet, she said, "I've been so careful with my life . . . Everything in moderation, according to reason, never rushing ahead—like . . . some people." She looked pointedly at her brother.

"Moderation," Mark said, "is something to be thrown over, as a sign of commitment to a particular choice; to excess . . . You *are* careful. Careful has been the point, I thought. To consider the alternatives, by looking for reasons why people behave so oddly."

"When you come up with those reasons," she replied, "people depend on you ... If I didn't show up Monday morning, twelve psychotic kids would throw themselves against the wall."

"But that's a shrink's dream—the power of knowledge over people, over themselves. You planned it that way."

"If I did or didn't, there it is ... I don't have any choice now."

"Except to throw it all over," he repeated. "I think whatever you do is easily worth slight additional discomfort to twelve psychotic kids."

"Yes, perhaps. But that doesn't mean you cash them in—like chips. In which case I wouldn't be worth the shit they smear on the walls."

He looked at her. "Do they really?"

"Each one wants a part of me every day ... I expected a smart office with nice rugs and Queen Anne—not Snakepit."

Mark awoke twice that night and sat dazed on the edge of the bed, chasing the same elusive dream. As his mind cleared, as the shapes of the darkened room materialized, the dream fell into fragments, into the wisps, the odorless garbage of dreams. It seemed a secret he was keeping from himself. The only thing he could imagine repressing was dying and he assumed it was this. It was a train heard in the distance; not necessarily coming his way, though often it seemed to be getting nearer. Like a train, it seemed also still to be one he could stop and board, or let pass by. Death now had something to do with a cathedrallike, cavernous nineteenth-century railway station of steel and glass, the great Terminus of Life. Sunday morning, since Vita was there, he asked her.

"It's not that it's a railway station," she replied, "but that it's like a cathedral. But can't you remember more?"

"Only that everyone else knows but me, like a secret."

"If you dream it again, write it down; or tell Bill."

But then it didn't happen again. They talked about everything, in their robes, over pancakes and eggs. They would confront George about the beach house. Then their health. Vita wanted to know what, if anything, they were frightened of.

"Only the hospital," Bill said without hesitation. "It's dangerous in the hospitals, so far. Everyone dies."

"Yes, that's the nature of the disease."

"It's the nature of hospitals," he insisted. "The drugs are all too strong. Too gross. It's been like that from the beginning. People all die."

They sat on the dock with the cat, which lay obligingly across Vita's lap, purring. "Whatever you're doing," she said to the cat, "it seems to be working."

PART

FOUR

By the middle of August, nights were cold and they added blankets to the bed. Mist on the lake lingered later in the morning and, on the bank opposite, certain trees leapt out of the green in deadly color. Each morning, waiting for the fire to catch, Mark stood shivering in the big wooden room, each day more easily imagining the place in winter—the frozen, snowbound lake, barren stick-trees rising up the hill, a north wind blowing all day in the face of the lodge. Aside from the way they each felt, it was time to leave. Bill had completed the model of an illustration, in paper and wood, of the Seven Deadly Sins, and had looked up from it one day recently with an immediate sense of sudden boredom. Neither of them had seen their doctors in two months.

There had been developments. Apart from headaches and fatigue, they no longer seemed to be ill in similar ways. In the past weeks Bill had been affected, in the increasing damp and chill, by a small dry unproductive cough. Patches of white had appeared at the back of his throat. His appetite was gone, and his color. At night, despite the cold, and perhaps because of the extra blankets, he awoke in a sweat and in the morning sometimes seemed to have a fever. They had not brought a thermometer.

Mark felt none of this. But the lesions which for two years had been carefully farmed and excised had grown back, or had left dark tainted scars that looked nearly the same. For him it was all in the skin, with weals and lumps of five or six varieties—raised tumors filled with blood, dark flat smudges just below the skin, small red welts, paired purple spots like spilled ink, deeper, palpable pea-shapes, hard and movable, too deep in the flesh to see; a raised mole had come up one night suddenly, like a mushroom, beneath the hair on the back of his head, a hard beaded little shape just outside the skull. Much of the bottom of his right foot was purple. The disk in the fascia below his sternum was larger. A small mark like a purple lentil had appeared one day on the point of his cheekbone, but over the next few days had then faded away, like a warning. He could still look in the mirror and pretend he was unaffected; but naked, with all these spots lighted up by the hot water and steam of his bath, his body was a map of disease. He knew from what he could feel here and there beneath the surface that it had gone all through him and would not stop.

They did not, or could not express to each other, beyond looks, the feeling of separation to be guarded against; as if at some time in the past—in a moment on the lake, or the terrace in Rome, at the top of the house in Cape May, or before that, even before they'd met—something to separate them had been interposed; or that two paths, running parallel at first, now forked off in different directions, neither leading to anything better than the other, but worse for being separate. It was this they fought against as much as illness or metaphor, that they not leave or be left alone.

The black cat had disappeared on a Saturday in late July; it had never come back, though they still looked for it, and Mark called out puss-puss each morning from the door. They thought someone had let it into their car and driven away. It had not died, a cat like that.

☆

August 17 Fla

Darling

The things you see and hear. Mum lately can't be moved so instead of bringing her home I spend those two days, or most of them, at the nursing home with her. The things they say to each other, the cries for help, the sorrow. If someone is quiet it is because they are doped or mute with rage. Mum would rather die. She warns that even one more day will drive her mad, then when I go back she's still alert, still waiting, angry as hell. She says if only she could die, if only I would shoot her, smother her with a pillow; anything. I know I would be crazy by now too, except who would notice? The rest of the time I sit here with this corpse of a novel, or mow the lawn. Mrs Ruggeri next door says if I don't remove the new trees immediately she will call the police and have them ripped out—I have interrupted her view of the lake. Mrs. Ruggeri disapproves of Mum being sent away, since she fears the same for herself, though she would not dare say anything to my face. Instead she complains about the trees. Furthermore, while I did not actually run over her little dog with the lawnmower, I did catch it with a wheel, producing a high-pitched mewling squeal commensurate with its size, which Mrs Ruggeri heard and perhaps even saw with her own piggy eyes. My satisfaction must be that she too, though still hale as seawater, will one day wind up in the same dreadful place as Mum.

These things conspire. So it's natural I should want to get away, merely to be rid of it, for some relief. Mrs Ruggeri is right. I did try to run over her dog. I did cut off her view with my trees, though I was simply trying to cut off our view of Mrs Ruggeri. This is what I remember of Fred's Lake—the privacy, the utter quiet and peace, the calm. A lake of one's own, a lake with a view. And yet. And yet and yet—when the wind comes up in the morning, and it's clear and cool, and the clouds come whipping across and it's all new—you think, this is why. And the perfect teen-gods on their bicycles, the apparently especially selected delivery men; the feeling that I am out of harm's way merely because it is so far from the nearest available penis. Because this is where we wound up, this is where I naturally belong. How arbitrary—but I think arbitrary is the point. No one and nothing ever planned this. Of course you will agree the universe is merely something that happened, as opposed to something that didn't.

Sis will be here this week for a few days, allowing me to get away without cutting the string—I just can't do that to Mum. You remember perhaps my mentioning a gay group in Austin looking for the planet Mary. I sent them a check for not much and they wrote back inviting me to come to Austin and see their operation. They have sent copious brochures, background papers on key people (principally rich former hippies) and the known facts about their destination—the star Sirius.

I'm Sirius and they are Sirius and I'm going. At any rate, it's free. Do not break the flow. Will be gone for just the weekend.

(Mrs) Neil Armstrong

Mark wondered if the idea of going to Sirius, indeed if the idea of going to Austin, was real or metaphorical. And just because they were all gay did not mean they weren't also crooks or crazy. The promise of a trip to outer space sounded like the promise of a cure for baldness. One certainly wanted to believe in it.

In the meantime they speculated. "We could send a check. Maybe they would ask us to Austin."

But Mark did not think Matthew meant he would actually go to Sirius. It was, instead, one of two things: his novel, or a form of suicide.

"A form of suicide?"

"A metaphor. He's thinking about it." This seemed logical since he was watching his mother die. They read the letter again. '. . . merely to be rid of it all, for some relief.'

But really, Bill thought, he was only going to Austin—something unknown and original to replace the all too certain and sad nursing home. And as Matthew himself had pointed out, it was free. Two days later, checking the post office one last time on their way back to New York, a second letter was waiting.

They *are* going. And they are taking along a few people who either very much want, need, or deserve to go—all gay of course. Not exactly a weekend in the country, it's dangerous, and depends on rather a lot. But there is a lot of money behind them, the best minds, the best gay minds of our time. However, let's face it, the idea is extreme. But my dears, an adventure. There exists, almost, the technology to do it all—with the small exception of a little thing called Fusion, but they expect to have that too within three years—They're called the Lambda Project and they believe if we don't do it now, before the nuclear mess, the colonization of Space will be set back a thousand years. Support systems necessary for such an undertaking go far beyond technology. They require the higher levels of achievement of an entire society, and a reasonably healthy Earth—which soon, they argue, we will no longer have. After the bombs drop not even your toaster will work. And how long, in years, in generations, in centuries, before we have the resources and the will to try again . . .

"This is make-believe," Mark said as they drove away. "On someone's part. And very elaborate. Unhinged, don't you think?"

"And if not?" Bill said. "Suppose it's real."

"How could it be? Things are not that far along yet. It's still science fiction."

"How do you know?"

"Have you heard anything lately about fusion?"

"That doesn't mean they're not close."

"Billy, after the Challenger, there is no space program."

"But this is private, not government . . ."

"You are biased in favor of the impossible," Mark said, his hands firmly gripping the wheel.

"—Not the impossible, the unlikely. There's also the magical."

"This is not magical, it's madness. It's a queen out of control."

"You don't know that, Mark. Suppose for a moment that fusion is possible . . ."

"But it isn't."

In Manhattan, in Fred's apartment, Bill awoke in the middle of the night with a high fever and drenched with sweat. By morning he had been admitted to the same hospital where Fred had been treated, in an identical room in the isolation ward. All doors here were marked in red, with warning signs to doctors, nurses, orderlies and visitors: gloves, masks and gowns required. Everything that came into the room bore a red diagonal stripe—for destruction—slashed across it. Mark asked at the nurses' station if this was to protect the patient or everyone else.

A large black woman bursting with color and health said, "That depends. It's really for everyone else. Some people like to glove up, others don't much care."

Bill had terrible headaches and lay in a daze or sleeping. Mark held his hand for hours at a time. When the doctors, one after another, asked Mark to leave for various examinations, he refused. The waiting room was filled with cigarette smoke. Everyone on the corridor but Bill had private nurses who sat watching their charges like flames in the wind, or bombs about to explode, or leaking boats, or sick gerbils: reduced or lower forms of life of questionable value. Bill awakened and wept from weakness in Mark's arms.

"What will happen?" he asked.

"Nothing. We'll get through this."

The clear silvery medicine dripped into his vein. During a bronchoscopy his left lung collapsed. The doctor apologized. Bill could not catch his breath. The small simple coughs were now long painful spasms. The lung must reinflate by itself or they would have to operate, going in as through the bulwark entrance to a locked house, through a flap opened in the chest.

Mark came back alone to Fred's, now Bill's, apartment and out of fear, loneliness, anxiety, and habit, rearranged the furniture in all the rooms. This took some time and effort, exhausting him enough to sleep through most of the night. The next morning the headaches were just as severe. They went on with the X rays and tests so that for long periods Mark sat alone in the empty room. They brought Bill back asleep and Mark sat by his side holding his hand. The doctor came in, without gloves or mask. "It's not too bad," he said. "We got the pneumonia early. But the collapsed lung is dangerous. If it hasn't reinflated in two or three days, we'll go in."

Mark now badly needed sleep and some sort of company to spell him at the hospital. They gave him the name and number of an agency that provided a different full-time nurse every eight hours around the clock. He went through five women to get three regulars, one of whom—a sweet elderly efficient white woman—set the standards for the other two, producing a vacuum to clean the fungus at the back of Bill's throat, changing the sheets without waking him, helping him to eat, gently massaging his back and neck.

Aside from his married niece Sarah, Mark knew several people in New York but none he would share all this with. He had called Vita, and she, Tessa, and Aunt Rose came up on the fourth day. Hugging them in the hall, he nearly swooned with relief at the affection they brought, not for the way they felt but for who they were, who they all had been together. "Oh my god, Vita, this is awful."

Tessa had brought flowers and a book, magazines and candy, and a scrawled note from Mara—all the talismans she could think of, including relayed messages and get-well wishes from everyone. Suddenly, like an arriving army, an entire family assembled itself again around him.

"Doesn't Bill have anyone?" Rose asked, looking around.

"Parents dead. A brother somewhere . . . I don't want the complications."

"Well, he has us," she said. And Vita said, "What can we do?"

"Sit with him. Just be there. He can't talk much, but just having you . . ." Mark took a deep breath. His stomach turned and he steadied himself against the corridor wall. He looked at Vita. "Who thought this up?" he said.

Bill smiled and held out his hand to them. Fearlessly, they kissed his cheek, having seen the warnings and somehow—in a way Mark would never afterward get over—ignoring them. Tessa said, "I want you back at Cape May for a rematch, immediately." And he smiled again and whispered, "It's a deal."

Rose said, "Are you in pain?"

"Can't breathe," he whispered, and Mark put his hand lightly on Bill's chest.

"It must reinflate," he explained. "We're praying to the air spirits . . ."

"The air faeries," Bill said weakly.

They stayed overnight at the apartment, which they

found large but strange and dusty, and next day did the laundry and shopped for groceries, vacuumed, did the bathrooms and kitchen floor. Vita said it was a relief to be useful. After another visit with Bill they took the train back to Philadelphia.

X rays each day showed slight improvement in the collapsed lung. On the eighth morning, when Mark arrived, Bill was sitting up, smiling. The oxygen tube was gone from under his nose and his voice had support.

"What happened?"

"The faeries were here. We inflated."

Mark shut the door and lay down on the bed, cuddling Bill to his chest. "Oh yes," Bill sighed. "Hold me." After a moment he said, "Don't you think this is a good sign?"

"What?"

"This." He threw back the covers to expose an erection. Mark grasped it.

"A definite sign of life . . . Where's the nurse?"

"Lunch . . . Maybe it's the medicine. Sometimes, for a few minutes, energy comes rushing through me."

"So I see." Mark lowered himself and put his mouth on it. Bill groaned with pleasure. In a few minutes he came and Mark sponged his belly and chest, both of them grinning with sheepishness and pride.

"That makes me feel so much better," Bill said with a sigh which, being too deep for his stricken lungs, made him cough. "But hungry."

"New York is your restaurant. Name it."

"Japanese . . . miso soup, sashimi, raw vegetables, strawberries . . ."

When he returned with the food, Bill was fast asleep,

the nurse in the chair by the window, beneath the flowers from George and Claudia, watching him sleep. She got up and took his pulse; he sleepily opened his eyes and closed them again, not waking. She was the fearless, efficient one—no mask, no gloves. She smiled at Mark. "He's better," she said. "If they're going to get through it, they come back in the first few days." Mark nodded to encourage her. "He has the strength, you can see it," she said. ". . . There's a boy down the hall." She stopped and shook her head. "And no one to visit him." She said the room number. When she had sat back down Mark went along the corridor to the closed door; he knocked lightly and went in. The lights were out and shades drawn, and the air smelled of oxygen, or something like ozone—a stuffy, sweet smell. The boy's bedlight was on, and Mark saw the face— swollen, purple around the puffy eyes, which were open and regarding him. But Mark could see, even with the discoloration and swollen cheeks, vestiges still of youth and beauty.

"Yes?" the boy said.

"I'm with my lover down the hall. Can I get you anything?"

"Thank you," he replied. "You can get me a new life."

"I wish I could." Mark came closer.

"Your lover . . . Does he have It?"

Mark nodded. "In Four fourteen."

"He's lucky to have someone."

"The nurse said you were alone . . ."

"They put me here at least—instead of Bellevue. I guess I should be grateful. For a while I was on the streets."

"Who are they?"

"My so-called family. They pay the bills but they're frightened to come. Better if they don't. They're awful people."

Mark took his hand. "How do you feel?"

"I'm dying . . . I feel it each day. It comes into the room, when I'm alone. It slips away when they come in . . ."

"What does?"

"Death. Sometimes I see it in people's eyes. They look at me and it's death looking down." He looked up closely at Mark. "Oh God," he said, squeezing Mark's hand, "to have someone who's not terrified of touching me . . . Are you . . . are you sick too?" he asked.

"Yes," Mark replied, startled. "We both are. He's got pneumonia."

"I've had that four times. That one's easy. They can keep a hamburger alive around here . . . But you're sick too?"

"Not so much. I'm all right. It's not my turn yet."

"Everyone will die. That's my consolation sometimes. When I think that everyone passing in the hall, or coming in here, even the doctors and nurses, the smug orderlies who look like they'll live forever, and act like it . . . All of them deader than doornails."

"I hope not," Mark said.

"You do?" The boy looked up at him in sudden anger, widening his blackened eyes. "Your lover will die, then you will; then all of them, one after another."

"Maybe not," Mark said quietly.

"Why not? Do you know some magic way? Are you any different from everyone else? Are you any better?"

"I won't die," Mark said. "Neither will my lover."

"Fuck you," the boy snapped. "It's better to die anyway . . . This slimy, evil world; this cesspool, this stink and slime. I never had a life. I'm twenty-three."

Mark squeezed his hand. "I'm sorry."

"I know . . . I'm sorry, too. I apologize. You're in it too. You know . . . But wait, till they all know. Till it's too late. When they've waited too long, thinking it was just us. So holier than thou. So much better than us. What a joke. What a wonderful joke! When someone hands them the bill. When they all die like flies, like me—of old age and boredom."

"Relax now," Mark said. "I'll come in again."

"I'll be dead," the boy replied. "I want to die. I'm so bored lying here. It hurts all the time."

"Do you want the nurse?"

"I want another life. I want what I didn't have. Ask her for that, the stupid cunt."

"Good-bye," Mark whispered.

The boy still gripped his hand. "I'm sorry. I hope you don't die," he said. "Or your lover. I'll tell them when I get over . . . What's his name?"

"Bill."

"Bill. I'll remember. And yours?"

"Mark."

"Bill and Mark. I'll tell them."

When he came back into the room Bill was sitting up, alone, going through the paper bag of Japanese food, removing little containers one by one. "Ummm, still warm." Mark came over and put his arms around Bill's neck, falling into tears, shaking with silent shivering sobs. "Poor baby," Bill said, holding him. "It's all

right, it's all right. I feel so much better. It's all right
. . . I love you so. Little one."

☆

New York Labor Day

Matthew

Would be calling you—so much to say—but
I don't want to put you off the telephone completely with raw, undigested news of this variety.
B in the hospital with pneumonia—il y a two
weeks, since the night we returned from the lake
a million years ago. He's responding to the drug,
and will be out in another two weeks, approx.
How terrible the hospital is, especially isolation.
My first time seeing this part of it; and having
it be Bill in the midst of such suffering and slow
dying—the tubes and carts, the linoleum and
flowers, the robotic nurses and so-calm doctors,
the centerfold orderlies. How you get to hate it.
Very like your nursing home except of course
everyone is under forty, and perfectly aware.
He has been wonderfully strong and brave, doing
and saying all the right things, being positive—
I'm the one who cries, but not often and only
because I pity us sometimes and think about the
life we should and would be living—as newlyweds
with the world to play in. But instead of pro-
found happiness, we have in each other survival.
I'll take it. Happiness comes later, after the cure,
a long normal life together, until the two of us
look and sound like Sam Jaffe in Lost Horizon.

But of course not you. You will be on Sirius eating frogs. We got the last letter the day we left the lake, and then all this happened. But now, as the dust settles, it is obvious once more—as it was for a few moments after reading your letter—just how dotty you are. Is it fear of It? Is it the horror of writing books? Middle age? Mrs Ruggeri? Is it my breath? We would all like to get away, even to get out. We all have our fantasies. Mine is being a blond, while you seek the planet Mary. I assume you have been joking—the way writers joke, for twenty pages at a time—but Bill insists you are serious, I mean Sirius, and that only my earthbound practicality prevents me from believing. B wants it to be true. He wants you to go. I suppose he would even like us to go. But that's not because he believes it is really possible— the Fusion, the spaceship, the destination—but only because he knows what it represents, as an idea. We all know that. Salvation. A better place. Something after. Play orchestra play. But darling if only believing could make it so. Then buggers like you and me would ride. I won't give you the lecture on Fusion, or play you the videotape of Challenger going bye-bye. Vita says that on one level space travel is just escapism. Thank you, Doctor, we knew that. But on another it is the actual destiny of humanity. As in the past, a few people will migrate. Vita points out that these migrations have never been initiated in large numbers. They are saying now that everyone in the world is descended from one female in Africa whose progeny took a hike. So, humans in space, if there aren't already humans elsewhere, and I doubt it, must come from Earth; and that means a few must go, or can go, depending on your attitude.

I know it's not tomorrow; that they must first get the Fusion machine working—and this sounds like more than three years. So there's time to discuss it. For now let me say: Because you want to go does not mean you can go. We will have to ask your father. So much could happen. It might rain. You might at the last moment prefer to be on the Best Seller List, or live in Oyster Bay. I don't blame you for wanting it, but for believing it to be possible. Someone is lying, or exaggerating. Or dreaming. I would think the only way for us to leave this planet is for someone to come and get us . . .

It had been the custom for years that everyone in the family come to Cape May for Labor Day weekend, even George and Claudia. On Saturday, while Bill was out of the room for X rays, Mark called the house. Tessa answered.

"Mark!" she said, "I was just going to call."

"Who's there?" he asked.

"Oh, everyone."

"Nearly everyone," he corrected.

"Well, that's what I mean."

"Did Dad come?"

"Yes, with guess who? Janet Delbono. Coming in from the porch this morning with a tray of dishes, she dropped the whole thing. Six plates of Mom's white china. A great beginning. She's nervous to begin with, but that destroyed her . . . When is Bill getting out?"

"Two weeks, if his lungs are clear. We'll come down there. When are you all leaving?"

"Monday, but Vita'll stay till Tuesday morning, and go to work from here."

"Did Sarah come?" he asked after a moment.

"Sarah? No."

"So she's here in New York."

"As far as I know . . ."

"Is George fishing?"

"No, he's here . . . Listen, hon, take care. Give Bill my love."

George came on. "Mark," he said, "I'm so sorry about Bill. How is he?"

"Better. Please thank Claudia for the flowers."

"How are you?"

"Tired. George, I want to talk to Sarah. Is she here in New York?"

"They went to Dan's parents for the weekend. She'll be back Monday."

"Did you talk to her?" Mark asked.

"Did I talk to her? Well, not exactly. She said something to Claudia after that weekend, but only in general, about the dangers; I mean the risks—to you and Bill—not to her or the baby . . ."

"Is that why they didn't come this weekend? Because you told them not to?"

"No, they had his parents . . ."

"What did you tell her?" Mark asked again.

"Look, you have enough to worry about, with Bill."

"Yes," Mark snapped. "Without your making it worse."

"Well, just forget about it. Sarah's fine. She's all wrapped up in herself and her baby."

"You mean, stay away from her. Is that what you're saying?"

"No, of course not. Just that it has not been put into words. I think she knows, because she's so close to you. But we haven't said it out loud."

"What a comfort you are, George."

"Look, what do you want? You don't want me to come right out and tell her, but you expect her to know."

"I want to know what you've said to her. Because that's different."

"Well, nothing; in so many words. And you know, she will wonder why the hell she wasn't told in the first place. My ass is grass."

"Your ass is grass anyway, George," Mark observed.

On Tuesday he called Sarah's apartment on West 89th Street. She had thought they were still in Massachusetts. "What are you doing in New York?"

"Bill's in the hospital, with pneumonia."

"Oh Mark, not *the* pneumonia."

"Afraid so."

"Oh Mark, I'm sorry. Are you there now? I'll come right over."

"No, honey," he said. "Meet me tonight for dinner. Just you. We have to talk."

She gave him a big hug. He said, "I have it too." And still holding him, not letting him go, she said, "I know." And when they drew back she had tears in her eyes. "Mark," she said, "I don't know how you could

— 173 —

think that it would make any difference. Or even scare me. I love you."

He hugged her again and they sobbed in the street, but it was New York and no one more than glanced at them.

"It was all too much in the beginning. I couldn't handle your knowing too. Your father is such a dork."

"Mark, he's scared."

They went into a restaurant, near the hospital, which was not much. Even with tears in her eyes, Sarah was young and radiant, clear fresh skin and eyes, her blondish hair just washed and fluffy.

"How do you feel?" she said, shedding her jacket onto the seat.

"I'm still okay. Though I don't know why. I think I'm supposed to be dead by now."

"But you don't even look sick . . ."

"I've got marks all over me you can't see."

"You do?"

"Bill has the other kind—the lungs, headaches. All inside."

"You should have told me. I could have helped you. Have you been here all alone?"

"Tess and Vita came for a few days."

"God, I hate being in the dark."

"I wanted to tell you at the beach. And then I couldn't by phone, or leave it to your parents."

"Well, they sort of told me, without telling me; enough to make me wonder. I guess I knew something was wrong when you wouldn't hold the baby. The only thing I worried about, for some reason, was his little friends at nursery school biting him. Isn't that stupid?"

They went up together to Bill's room, though Mark did not think this necessary since Sarah had met him just the once at Cape May. But she insisted, and kissed him when they came in. The next morning, in the same spirit, in her apartment, she unceremoniously dumped the baby in Mark's lap when the phone rang. When she hung up and turned back to them, Mark was weeping at the feel of this small, ineffably healthy treasure in his arms; at the gift his niece had given which, to her, as far as she knew, was no different than a possibly doomed offering of blood-sacrifice to the volcano god—the first such creature he had held or touched in two years. He thanked her, since to say nothing, he thought, would be impossibly ungrateful; and it seemed, for a moment, as the thought passed through her mind, that she suddenly weighed the possibilities for the first, not the second or hundredth time. She said, "Not touching him does so much more harm."

The baby felt rare and exorbitantly expensive; he looked up at Mark with long-lashed, blue-violet eyes, in complete trust and unconcern—only the privileged came this close, only the dear. Even Tessa had not gone this far with Mara, though Mara had been already of an age not to be put in anyone's lap not of her own choosing. Now suddenly Mark was free to play with him, on the thick rug, with his rubber rings and dolls; free to breathe his air and touch his toys, while Sarah made breakfast and Dan dressed for work.

In the third week Bill's IV was removed and he was switched to pills of the same drug. The headaches had stopped, he felt better, more energetic and fit than in the last few months—a temporary benefit to those who responded to the drug. Doctors referred to what was coming as the Honeymoon—ten or twelve months of improved, relatively normal health. When his lungs were clear he was allowed to leave the hospital. They spent the night at Fred's apartment, then drove to Cape May the following day.

The big house and garden bore the usual signs of a long, hectic summer, three months of kids, dogs, and guests. In Tessa's and Vita's cases, dinner each night had usually involved fifteen, and twice that on weekends. But a woman had come in to clean each week—except when Claudia was there because they had had words—and the gardeners saw to everything but the borders, which they were under strict orders from Mark not to touch; and now with the repositioning of the furniture and a little weeding, the place recomposed itself within a few days. It was a house so solid, so substantial it easily absorbed the abuse, the outright damage of all the Valerians at once. Primarily Mark found simple disorder—the closets, drawers, pantry, garage, storeroom. An awning had been ripped in a storm, a chair leg had come unglued, a shower drain was clogged, the living-room slipcovers were filthy. Bill watched him fly from one thing to another, cleaning and foofing, and the house, which even in disarray was handsome, resumed its usual perfection and sheen.

Mr Valerian's car turned into the long, tree-lined drive, a stately approach interrupted by a picket gate, which was closed. Mark was the only one in the family who bothered with it. As he drove the last few hundred feet, Mr Valerian again calculated the dollar value of all this. In that moment the house and garden had reached the height of their beauty, and thus perhaps of their worth. This day also had been one of those rare crystal events of which there were a dozen in every season, when the light as it fell at different angles cast everything into a succession of long, brilliantly lit moments; and the house, set up against the blue sky and sea, was traced with gold light in a super dimension of clarity; the colors of the lawn, garden, gravel and awnings punctuated by the sharp blue-white trim of windows and huge porch.

To Mr Valerian however, stepping from his car, the effect was not so much of perfection and readiness, as of worth. Much of his time had been devoted to deciding what to do next to raise money. He hated to part with any of it, but something must go—and soon—if he was to appease the banks and save the rest. He had decided that from his own point of view this house was the thing he would miss least and, of everything he owned, would bring the greatest financial relief. He often did things without first admitting them to himself; and if there was a specific reason for this visit, beyond seeing his son, it was to inform Mark of his intention to sell the house for as much as he could get.

The Court deal had been planned as the triumph of a career, the means for a luxurious old age—of traveling, of midrange weekend gambling in Atlantic City and Las Vegas, of the subsidy of odd impulsive projects and diversions. He would dabble, invest, study, indulge his new passion for cooking, which for him might easily involve the construction of a restaurant-size kitchen, or even a restaurant. He had hoped also to begin dividing his wealth among his children and grandchildren, so as to create, at the end, a feeling of generosity and largesse. Beyond providing them with a handsome upbringing and good schools, he had never indulged them, not by today's standards, and had thought to do it now with gifts and trusts.

Instead, cruelly, it seemed he might lose everything including, most specifically, his own independence and security in old age. He might have to leave the splendor of his own huge empty house; this he had thought to turn gradually into a sumptuous and most private nursing home, possible only with vast amounts of money. Now it seemed he must sell everything, not to insure his survival but simply to settle his huge debts. And where, after that, would he be left?

On the widow's walk atop the tower, where Mark and Bill had come for the light, they watched Mr Valerian's car wind up the drive. They had not known he was coming and Mark thought immediately of dinner. Mr Valerian stepped onto the porch and looked up and down, at the difference between this visit and the last, over Labor Day. As if declared dangerous, the beach was empty as far as he could see in either direction.

Mark heard his father call his name up the tall staircase that fell through the house in a cascade of white spindles and steps. At the bottom Mr Valerian looked up expectantly. "I thought I'd surprise you," he said as Mark came down. "Do you mind?"

"I'm delighted. How did you know we were here?"

"Tessa mentioned it . . . How is Bill?" he added, to show he had been completely briefed.

"Better. Is everything all right?"

"Oh yes. Just that I hadn't seen you in a while."

"Two months," Mark said. They shook hands.

"How are you?" his father asked in a formal greeting sparked by the touch of their hands.

"I'm fine. I feel fine."

"That'a boy." Mr Valerian looked around. "Can I get you something? Would you like a cup of tea?"

On the porch, the light slanting through the wings, they sipped their tea and watched the ocean, while Mark gave an account of the hospital and, after that, of the lake. Bill sat quietly, wrapped in a blanket, thinking that Mr Valerian looked nothing like Mark; and that, beyond this, there was nothing in one to make you think of the other.

"How did you find the house?" Mr Valerian asked.

"The usual odds and ends. Some water damage downstairs from a clogged drain in the shower. And a lot of beach towels are gone. They march off. But the girls may have them . . ."

Mr Valerian looked up at the porch ceiling, over their heads, which was peeling in blue tatters. "This looks pretty bad," he observed.

"He used the wrong paint," Mark said. "From the blue room, for Chrissake. I'll make him do it over. There's a couple of things like that. Not too bad."

"No, it all looks fine."

Bill excused himself and went upstairs to lie down until dinner.

"Pretty rough," Mr Valerian said quietly, when Bill had gone in. Mark shook his head. "Is that what you want to do?" his father asked. "—Get involved with someone who's . . . not well?"

"Dad . . ." They looked at each other.

"Oh I know. These things happen on their own. But with the two of you sick . . ."

"Well yes, of course," Mark said sharply. "You would just drop him, because he can't bale hay."

"No, I wouldn't. But you should have someone who can handle things—for you. Instead of having to take care of him."

"We take care of each other. And let me tell you," he said, turning in his seat and facing his father head on. "Let me tell you, things would be very different now if it weren't for Bill."

"What do you mean?"

"I mean, I can't even get your attention with a fatal disease."

"Now that's unfair," Mr Valerian said, as if to a third-party referee, shaking his head.

"Well what happened to your big speech about us going through this together? I haven't seen or heard from you in two months."

"But Mark, nothing's happened yet. You're still fine. And I'm here, aren't I?"

"Yes, you are. But a lot can happen in two months. And did."

"Well, you're not being fair, you know," Mr Valerian said in a calmer voice. "You didn't even have a telephone up there."

"What about the last three weeks in New York? No

calls, no nothing. 'How are you? Do you need any-thing?' Vita and Tessa came up. Even George sent flowers."

"Well I'm sorry. I apologize. You have to under-stand. This is the worst time of my life. I don't know what's going to happen. You have no idea . . ."

"Why do you say that? I know about it."

"No, you don't. No one does."

"It's hardly a secret the company's failing."

"Well you know, Mark, maybe it's a case of my running away from my problems a little . . . and trying to spare you the ugly details. You have your own troubles."

"You'll be a hundred and you still won't understand."

"Understand what?"

"The worst thing is being ignored."

"I was not ignoring you. I was sparing you. But I said I'm sorry. It won't happen again. I promise you."

Again Mr Valerian could not be persuaded to stay overnight, and again he offered the ready excuse of an early morning business meeting for which he must re-turn to Philadelphia. Because of this elusiveness, Mark at dinner raised the item of Janet Delbono.

"What about her?" Mr Valerian looked up from his plate, startled. He glanced at Bill. "She's fine."

"I understand you're—keeping company."

"Well." Mr Valerian reddened visibly, then recov-ered. "I wouldn't use that particular phrase."

"Why not? Isn't it a love affair?"

"Certainly not. I will never love anyone but your mother," Mr Valerian said flatly. "And that's that."

"Will you marry?" Mark asked, as if not having

heard, or as if having understood such a declaration to be meaningless rhetoric.

"Mark . . ." His father shook his head.

"What?"

". . . She's only recently widowed. And really, this is a question of companionship. I cannot see marriage as a possibility. To anyone."

Mark wanted to say, "That'a boy," but restrained himself. Instead he asked why not.

"Because. It's just not in the cards. She has her own life, her own family. She's already spread so thin. She's got four kids of her own, you know. There's so much too-ing and fro-ing. It wouldn't work . . . Besides," he said after a moment, "I like it the way it is now. I've gotten used to doing as I please, without explaining to anyone."

"There's two sides to that," Mark said. "It's also nice to have someone wondering where you are, and waiting when you get home."

"Oh yes. But I've done that, you know. It also has its drawbacks."

They had cleared away the dinner dishes, and it was nearly time for Mr Valerian to leave; sitting in the living room, he said, "Mark, I don't want to upset you, but it's time we faced facts. I can't hold all this together indefinitely, and it may be the moment to sell this place."

Mark only stared at him, not wanting to say anything to make it easier to discuss or ever resolve this issue.

"I know how you feel about it," Mr Valerian went on after a moment, "but I have to do something. It's all going to pieces . . ."

Mark sat wondering what would be the surest, most effective way of thwarting him. "This is where I came in," he said finally, getting up from the couch as if to leave.

"Well yes, I know. But it's different this time. The banks won't give me any more. Sales are still way down. I need something to carry us a while . . ."

"You mean you'll sell this place just to buy more debts . . . That's like throwing it away."

"I would like to be able to do it without selling anything. But I want you to understand—the banks won't give me any more, because they know I'm not worth any more. If I were to liquidate everything right now I would maybe have a few hundred thousand left over. And that wouldn't last long."

"So you've already borrowed against the house."

"Some . . . Nothing to speak of."

"Why don't you ever tell me the goddamn truth?"

"What does that mean?"

"You say if you liquidated everything you would have a few hundred thousand left over. But this place is worth a fortune. So which is it?"

"I've borrowed against it, yes. I had to. I've done it before and if I had to I'd do it again."

"What you're saying is that this house is already gone," Mark said bitterly.

"That's what I'm trying to tell you. Unless something happens, we could lose it all."

They sat a few minutes in silence, until Mr Valerian spoke again in a quieter, conciliatory tone. "Well look. We haven't got to the end yet. And I'm a fighter, goddamn it. I'm not going to give up."

Mark said nothing. The house was utterly quiet, like

a pet that knows when to keep out of the way. He thought yes, not only was his father a fighter, but he enjoyed having his back to the wall, enjoyed the exhilaration of the gambler down to his last chips—a position familiar to and easily understood by those who had started with nothing. There was even something in it of the symmetry and easy appeal of ending up with nothing. Rather than exhausting or crippling Mr Valerian, it seemed, at seventy-five, to be rejuvenating him. This was tenacity, of course, Mark thought—the wily tenacity of those whom others have long since counted out. His father knew that if he held on long enough, through enough change, through the ruin and death of others, through enough simple revolutions of the planet, anything might happen: reversals, setbacks, breakthroughs, triumphs. Only tenacity, only survival, countered wretchedness and failure. Only hanging on.

☆

September 15 Loch Mess

Dear Mark

Not having heard, assumed some hideousness had ensued, though it does not from your letter sound as bad as could have been feared. And now Bill is better, and out of hospital, which was fast. (Will send a copy of this to New York, though imagine you have made a beeline to Cape May.) Darling are you all right? Can you cope? do you want me to come up? Life has become so—medical. And I do feel responsible for you two, but don't want to be alarm-iste.

Must learn, watching all of this—including Mum and friends—that in the long run we will get through. If one didn't believe this, it would be better to flip the sign in the window to Closed.

There's about to be a miracle—one of those events that change everything. And aren't we due? I bring this up here and now because, really, it also concerns you both; or should. If Bill has moved into the next phase, all the more reason to think about joining me—us—the Project. I believe they would have you, though it might cost serious money, I mean Sirius money.

But what miracle? you ask.

Some years ago, at the beginning of the project, Lambda did something wonderful, something intuitive and direct—something only gay girls would think of: on the days of the Dog Star, the dog days of August, they aimed one of the world's most sophisticated radio transmitters at Sirius each morning for a week. The broadcasts included a statement of our existence here, enough information to decipher the language, and a request. The request was, "Will you receive us?" Only well-brought-up homosexuals would be so polite. Few in the project gave the idea much importance because radio waves, even when electronically enhanced, travel at such comparatively slow speeds. But it was inexpensive and easy, so it was thought worth trying. That was six years ago, in August 1981.

As it has been explained—was going to say 'revealed'—to me, there has been one basic assumption underlying the whole Lambda Project:

a belief in the history of a past connection between a planet in the Sirian system and Earth's ancient Egyptians. To be sure, the connection was completely one-sided, with an almost slavish attention on the part of the Egyptians to Sirius and the Sothic cycle. Rituals, religion, calendar, social and agricultural schedules—all of it related directly to Sirius. (I am summarizing whole packets of Lambda literature here) The question is, how and why did a Sothic obsession originate? Why base an Earth calendar on a star cycle of nearly fifteen hundred years? Why go to such lengths in orientation—physically, spiritually, architecturally? The answer, the assumption, is that the Ancient Egyptians *were* Sirians. I say assumption because none of it could be proved. It was a leap of faith.

You must at this point suppress an apparently universal prejudice, a cultural, religious, visceral feeling of skepticism, even cynicism, regarding these matters: other planets, aliens, space travel, UFO-ology, science fiction. How people's eyes glaze over. Perhaps it is the still apparent gap in technology—the unlikelihood of being able to leave the solar system, much less cover huge distances of interstellar space—that make most people dismiss the possibility as unreal (a word like unclean) and fantastic—speculative nonsense. There is in it too the notion of godlessness, taboo, ignorance and fear. Get over it. It is simply new.

All members of the Project are sworn to secrecy; so please, as we used to say, Burn This.

Your lips are sealed. Still, the story can hardly be contained indefinitely—there are too many people involved, most of them gossip-loving fagoons. But, for now, this is secret stuff. I am telling you because I want you both to come with us, because you must be able to make an informed decision about it.

You will of course have questions and I expect you will write or call immediately, but first I wanted you to get used to several ideas, including the one about you and Bill selling up and coming with us. I so want this to sound sane and logical; does it?

And the radio message? Lambda people calculate it has taken most of the six intervening years for it to reach the Sirian system, and only three days for their reply to reach us. Yes, their reply. Lambda is now studying the possibility of it having been faked—only fakery could compensate for such speed—three light years in as many days. But then it does not appear that we or anyone else have the technology even to fake the reply—a message as if received from deep space. Not to mention the contents.

"They would be delighted." It was all quite true about the Egyptians. They came here, as they went to many other places, while the smaller of their two suns ignited four thousand years ago. Subsequently, they were able to return to their planet, which is called Splendora (they believe) in our language. "Bright lovely being," they suggest, would be another way of putting it.

*　　*　　*

I will not apologize for any of this. Take it or leave it. It is all true. I am aware of the implications, the difficulties, even the inconsistencies. But there it is.

Just as they have been able to boost the radio signal in our follow-up transmissions, that is, boost them from their end, they say they can tractor and boost our ship and guide it to Splendora. Forget the Fusion machine, forget guidance and landing systems, forget six years asleep in space—problems which were going to delay us for years. They are able to eliminate distance, space itself; so that the speed of anything is enhanced—even the speed of light. Think of hyperspace, though it is really one of the other dimensions. As it says in my rearview mirror, 'Objects are closer than they appear.'

There is more every day. They have shown us a way to send pictures, diagrams, plans—to use the computers, in fact. The delay in transmission is shorter and shorter. Each reply brings a quantum leap of information. They do not mind if we share it with the Government, but Lambda is wary of being shouldered aside, so the secrecy is on our end. However Lambda is certainly being monitored. It is a matter of opinion and conjecture, with the Project, as to what has been overheard, and what can be understood by eavesdropping, Government or otherwise. After that, I don't understand.

We have told them of the Plague. They say

these things must be worked out on our own, to prevent false developments which then might subsequently collapse. However they will cooperate in any way we wish among those who have the intention of making the journey to Splendora.

They equate the impulse to leave Earth with the actual accomplishment. Thus their help and cooperation, though they will not as you suggest actually come and get us. We are not the first to make contact, as our planet was not the only temporary refuge of their civilization. We are neither the first nor the last to track the clues. Simply however the best-looking. We have exchanged pictures, like a dating service. You would say they are *gracile*—long, lean, delicate, in the sense of a swimmer's body as opposed to a fullback's—but essentially humanoid (rather than insectoid or plant-like or fishy). They have expressed pleasure in our looks, with a definite preference for men. Darling they *are* gay. Reproduction something of a mystery.

That should do.

Matthew

"What's he going to do with his mother?" Mark said, putting the letter aside. "Stuff her?"

"He might take her along. If they could help us, they might rejuvenate Mum."

"There is no 'they.' He's simply finishing his novel."

"Is that what you think," Bill said. "He's making it all up?"

"Splendora. Hyperspace. May we be real for a moment?"

" 'The eyes glaze over,' " Bill said. "He's right about the prejudice. No one wants to believe in this sort of thing. But it's stupid to think we won't one day travel to the stars. In fact it's arrogant to feel we shouldn't or that, out there somewhere, others aren't already darting about like tourists."

"So where are they?" Mark asked.

"I'm sorry, but I think all these unexplained UFOs are simply startled creatures passing by, and only trying to avoid the place. You notice they don't tend to stick around . . . Sirius is the closest major star—practically minutes away. In fact they would be the most logical first contact. And here they are."

"—No. We don't know that," Mark interrupted. "Here Matthew is, with a delicious story."

"I'll say."

". . . So buy his novel."

"Mark, I buy it all. He's not kidding. It's real."

"Stop. You do not know that."

"If this were fantasy he would say so . . . Shouldn't we call? If he has simply gone off, you could tell from the sound of his voice."

". . . Too neurotic too long for a voice check."

"What about the Lambda literature he mentions?" Bill said. "That could be proof."

"Not really; just proof of the extent of Matthew's fantasy."

One day in the following week Mark drove alone to Philadelphia for an appointment with Dr Thompson.

The first thing he noticed when he came into the office was that Theo's mustache had gone white.

"Did we do that to you?" Mark asked, sitting down.

"Do what?"

"Didn't it used to be blond?" He touched his own upper lip. Thompson smiled. "No, actually I just stopped coloring it."

"You never, in your wildest hippocratic dreams, imagined any of this . . ."

"No, we didn't."

They exchanged a look of what seemed and felt, to Mark, like affection. The white mustache added years to Theo's looks. Mark had thought himself the older of the two; now he wasn't sure. "Are you all right?" he asked.

"Fine. I've been very busy. Last night . . ."

"What?"

". . . was a bad night. Never mind that. How are you?"

"I'm all right, aside from some new lesions."

"No cough, no fever?"

"No."

"Bowel movements?"

"I'm very proud of my bowel movements."

"You should be, at this point. How's Bill doing?"

"He's with me in Cape May."

"I called his doctor . . . Good response to the drug."

"All in a matter of a few weeks."

"Those who get through it fast do better."

"The honeymoon . . ."

Theo stood up. "Let's go inside."

On the way to the examining room Mark, as usual, stepped onto the scale. In two years he had gained thirty pounds—two pounds or less at every visit. He had leveled off at 190, though even today he was another pound heavier.

"I would stop," Theo said. "I would try to keep my lips together."

"It's armor," Mark replied. "It's a sable coat." Something to lose if he couldn't eat.

In the examining room, with Mark stripped to his underwear, Theo began by taking his blood pressure. Over their shoulders they watched the thin column of mercury slide down the tube and begin to beat with his heart. "One forty over eighty," Theo announced. He looked into Mark's mouth with a light, checked the glands in his neck, listened to his back, then ran his hands over each and all of Mark's lesions—to feel which were raised and which were flat. But to Mark the touch was light, magical, almost electric, beyond erotic.

"Some new ones," Theo remarked, "but nothing dramatic. All very stable, I'd say." Mark lay back and Theo palpated his liver and spleen, pushing here and there; felt the glands under his arms and in his groin. "Okay, Mark. Get dressed and come into my office."

When he went back into the room Theo was writing in Mark's file. "Why do you think . . ." Mark began. "Why, after all this time, aren't I getting any worse?"

"Hard to say."

"How many others do you have left like me?"

"Three or four," Theo replied, still writing.

"There used to be more."

"I'm not sure why, of course. It may be that some people lack a co-factor. Or they have a genetic difference, some extra strength they've inherited. Probably both."

"Then doesn't it seem logical something would work on me before it would on others?"

"Logical, yes; but not certain."

"Is there anything you would think of giving me at this point?"

Theo stopped writing and regarded him a moment over the desk. "There comes a need sometimes," he began, "a need to take something. It's the feeling that if something isn't done . . ."

"Yes, I feel that."

"It's more psychological than physical. I wouldn't want to interfere with what your body is doing for itself. We don't know what these drugs would do to your system . . ." He stood up and went over to the window, looking out either in consideration of the view or of what he was about to say to Mark; then came back and sat down. "There are very promising early reports of a treatment first started at Bethesda for cancer, involving the processed leukocytes of siblings, together with a modified form of interferon—very preliminary. It may only work for certain people, and it may not be permanent. It's a difficult course of treatment. Quite toxic. But they say downstairs they have had good early results . . . You have family . . ." Theo said.

Mark nodded. "A brother and two sisters."

"A good crop. And they would be willing to cooperate?"

"To give blood? I'm sure they would."

"Tell them to call for an appointment. And in the meantime, we'll give them a month or so downstairs to work things out."

He had arranged to have lunch at his father's house after the appointment but when he arrived, George's, Vita's, and Tessa's husband's cars were parked in the driveway. The only reason he could think of for this was that something had happened to his father. But everyone was in the kitchen when he came in.

"What's going on?"

"I wanted you all here," Mr Valerian said, "so we could iron out—this situation." Mark kissed his two sisters and shook George's and Neil's hands. "It seemed the easiest way," his father went on, "since you were already coming."

He led them into the huge living room, devised, as the whole house had been devised, on principles associated in the Valerians' minds with the baronial generosity of Hollywood stage sets; so that in every room, but especially in this one, you found wide expanses of empty floor, on which presumably you acted and lived. Here most of the good English furniture Mark had found lorded it over Margaret's sensible reproductions, the best from Sloane's, in groupings that suggested the breakdown of society into manageable numbers. A big, south-facing window behind the couch was filled with plants, and the sun, as they entered the room, had just arrived through the green. The effect was as if the director had obligingly hit the lights.

And since nothing here was ever different, Mark in the first few moments could only think of how, if allowed, he would turn the room upside down; thereby missing some of what Mr. Valerian had begun by saying.

"—meeting so that we can discuss this together, without anyone being left out."

Mark glanced at the other faces. All intently watched their father, except that as Mark looked at Tessa her gaze shifted to lock with his. 'The bullshit begins,' she said by widening her eyes.

Mr Valerian sat in his tall wing chair, the twin to one in which George sat across the room. Vita and Mark again occupied the couch, Tessa a chair in the curve of the piano, some distance away, with Neil beside her. Mr Valerian cleared his throat, and when he spoke again his voice cracked.

"I don't think you people quite understand the situation. Things are very bad at Marval, and they've been bad for some time. Unless we turn it all around, and soon, we may have to close the doors." He paused to let this idea have its effect. "Now I've already brought up the possibility, with Mark earlier in the week, of selling the beach house . . ."

"I want it understood immediately," Mark put in, "that I am opposed to selling the house as much as ever, and will never agree to letting it go."

"Well now, you see," his father replied, "that's just not an attitude we can afford right now."

"How much have you borrowed against it?" George asked smoothly, and Mr Valerian said, Six hundred thousand.

"It's not an attitude," Mark said. "It's the way I feel. It's the way I think you all should feel. It's certainly the way Mom felt."

"The point is to raise money," George said. "It's the logical thing to sell."

"Is that right?" Vita said. "I thought the point was to protect our interests. The beach house now seems to be worth more than Marval."

"That place can only get more valuable," Mark added.

"It's already worth considerably more than when you wanted to sell it two years ago."

"Yes, Mark, but do you know," George asked, "how much it costs to run? It's money Dad doesn't have right now."

"It's petty cash compared to his other expenses," Vita replied. "George," she looked up at him. "We know how you feel, or don't feel about this house. It's a huge dollar-sign to you. But we wonder about the wisdom of letting it go if the proceeds will just get dropped into the company. I mean at least this is something. But if it all goes for debts . . . I know Dad actually controls the house with a Life Interest, but Mom left it in our names, and it seems, now that we look closely, that this is just another of your schemes."

"Don't start, Vita," he said. "Just let me tell you up front that none of this matters to me one way or the other. At a twenty percent appreciation every year, the beach house is a solid investment. As far as I'm concerned we can keep it indefinitely. But it's expensive and already very valuable. Selling it now would be a solution."

"A solution on one hand," Mark said, "a disaster on the other. All you can think of is money and balance sheets. And even that wouldn't be bad if you were right. But you're not. You were wrong to want to sell it two years ago, and you're still wrong. But forget that. The real reason not to sell is the same as it's always been. *Us.* And I know I'm right and I'm not going to give in. And let me say something else—since I don't guess anyone else is going to say it . . . I have enough to worry about right now." He stood up. "I'm sick, goddamn it! And so is Bill. You know how I feel about this place, and still you push it. What is the matter with you! What do I have to do, crawl on my belly?"

"Mark," Mr Valerian said. "It's all right. Don't get yourself excited."

"Why the hell not! He would sell *me* if he could get a good price."

"Why do you say that?" George demanded. "This isn't my idea."

"Who says it isn't?" Mark pointed a finger at his brother. "You've been pushing Dad to sell this place for ten years. And you've been wrong! And you're still wrong. So lay off!"

George was shaking his head. Then he looked up. "I am so tired of being the heavy in this family . . ."

"Well, I suppose you think it's easy being the leader of this bunch. This will give you some idea," Mr Valerian said after a long silence. "I had hoped you could settle your differences, but it doesn't look like it."

"Pop," Vita said, "you say our differences. Where do you think you've been in all this—Toledo?"

"I'd like to think that when I'm gone you'll be able to work things out between you."

"Yes, fine. But you're not gone yet. And it's just as much your problem as ours. It's your house. It's your company."

"That's right, goddamn it! And don't any of you forget it."

"Dad . . ." Vita said.

"Well, I'm fed up with all of this. What you people can't seem to understand is that the whole goddamn mess is about to go under."

Till now Tessa and Neil had said nothing—Tessa seldom did in these situations—but now Neil shook his head and smiled, doing both for some time before speaking. Mr Valerian took the cue and turned in his direction.

"I know," Neil said to his father-in-law, "that you still have a great deal at risk, but I think there are already signs that things at Marval are turning around . . ."

"Oh, is that so?" Mr Valerian said sarcastically. "Perhaps you could explain that to the banks."

"Well, yes, I'd be glad to," Neil replied. "We have our own drill now. And there's no reason to think it won't do as well as the Court drill . . ."

"You can't sell drills without orders," George put in.

"That's right," Mr Valerian said. "I keep waiting for you guys to bring them in. But where are they?"

"That's just about to happen," Neil said confidently. "We just need a little more time."

"We don't have any more time," Mr Valerian insisted. "I am at the end of my rope."

Again there was a silence, which then was broken by Vita. "Mark," she said, turning to him on the couch, "would you agree to their taking a full mortgage on the house?"

"I'll agree to anything short of selling it . . . Yes, I would."

"Tessa?"

"Sure," she said, startled to be addressed.

Vita looked at her father. "Would that be enough, Dad?"

And Mr Valerian looked at George.

*   *   *

And then, in the kitchen, not yet saying good-bye but about to, Neil unwittingly touched a match to a longish fuse by observing that it was strange, or ironic, that Vita had never taken part in the running of Marval. And Mark said, "Yes, but she was, after all, just a woman," and smiled at Vita. And Mr Valerian got immediately angry and said that was nonsense—Vita had never shown the least interest in coming into Marval.

Then Mark said, "You didn't want me in there either—after you found out I was gay."

"That's not true!" his father thundered.

"Well, I assume it's true, since it all happened at once. I was going to start after college, then told you about myself and didn't start—all in the same few weeks."

"That's not the way it was," Mr Valerian said angrily. "It just shows what you know . . . You were the one who was supposed to run the whole thing."

"So why didn't I?" he asked.

"Because you didn't want to. Why do you think?"

"—For the same reason as Vita—because I was just a woman," Mark said evenly.

"That's a lot of shit!" Mr Valerian was now red in the face. "She never cared about it."

"Neither did I." Mark looked at Vita and saw the look of alarm in her face.

"Well, you've got such a cock-eyed way of looking at things," his father said. "If that's what you think . . ."

"That's what I remember."

"Then you remember wrong, my friend. It was always my intention to make you president of the whole thing. But you had other ideas—like being a gardener . . ."

"You say that with such contempt—'like being a gardener.' Like being a Nazi. Because it wasn't what you wanted . . ."

"Why would I want my son, after all of this—" Mr Valerian with a gesture indicated the huge kitchen, the opulent house around them, "—why would I want my son to dig ditches?"

"What makes you think you can talk to me like that?" Mark said.

"I'll talk to you any goddamn way I please," Mr Valerian snapped back.

Mark said nothing, staring at his father.

"Then . . ." he began.

"Then nothing," Mr Valerian said brutally, turning in disgust.

Mark looked at George and Vita. George said later he was too shocked to react. Neil and Tessa had taken something out to the car. Tessa subsequently said she came back in to find everyone gaping and silent. She looked at Mark.

"What happened? What's the matter?"

Mark began to tremble, then vibrate. "Mark!" she cried. "What is it? Tell me!" She held his shoulders. She turned to the rest of them, all perhaps now realizing what was happening but not what to do about it. Even Vita seemed in a trance.

The trembling had become nearly a seizure, though he stood in one place, on his feet, without collapsing. From inside his body it felt like a severe thunderstorm, from within a shack—dry but barely dry, protected but buffeted by elements too huge to envision. Tessa clutched him to herself, her arms around his neck. Mark briefly became aware of the weight anchoring him to the spot. He took deep breaths and firmly removed her arms, calming himself, not to be calm but to free himself. He stepped back, trembling less, and looked at his father.

"You HATE ME!" he cried. "You're waiting for me to DIE!"

Mr Valerian practically stepped back in surprise. Vita said later she thought in this moment that Mark would hurt himself, or his father, and looked at the knife rack on the counter nearby. Still no one moved.

"WHY AM I STILL HERE?" Mark screamed at him. "WHY DON'T I DIE!" He looked at his father. "Isn't that it!"

The trembling had begun again and he hugged himself, but from within this vibrating shell he saw the expression on his father's face had changed. The anger, the puffed proud aggressive anger was gone, and in its place were the simplicity and pallor of shock.

"YES!" he screamed in his father's face. "You're scared! But only for yourself! NOT FOR ME!"

He turned and collapsed in on himself; at least that was the feeling. Actually he leaned against the refrigerator. "No one's there," he said. "You never were."

Then George was talking to him. Mark heard the voice for some time before he was aware of what it was saying, on and on in a long drone, the tone of which, rather than any sense of the words, seemed to attract his attention, like a tap on the shoulder, or the insistent but quiet repetition of his name; until at last Mark thought to listen, as one does to the lyrics of a song, to see if the words apply in some way to oneself.

". . . It's all right, Mark," George was saying, over

and over. "Just relax and take a few deep breaths . . . It's all right. We're here . . . It's all right. Just try to relax . . . I don't blame you. I don't see how you do as well as you have with all this pressure, this tremendous strain . . . fear and worry. But we love you, we're your family and we love you . . ."

Of which Mark heard, ". . . right, Mark . . . relax . . . deep . . . we're right. Just blame . . . your family . . . love you . . ." On and on, while George and Tessa led him into the den and sat on either side, Tessa with her arms around his neck again like a sea anchor in a storm, with George's voice droning on.

Mark looked up, into Vita's face a few feet away, and saw in her eyes what he hadn't in the others: the knowledge of hopelessness. Her eyes said, No lies, no compensations. She had not, from the beginning of his confrontation with his father until now, said a word. They looked at each other a long moment, until Mark's eyes flooded over again with tears. Still George went on. ". . . nothing is going to happen. It'll be all right . . ." And Mark understood that the feeling and intent behind these banalities and the look in Vita's eyes were the same: Would he get through this with them? Would they all grow old together?

George now, a few inches from his face, had stopped the droning accompaniment, and, with a change of voice, had moved on to the practical, the immediate. "I don't think you should be alone. Why don't you stay here tonight?"

Mark looked up at his brother with sudden contempt, and George immediately suggested he stay with him and Claudia.

"Bill is waiting for me in Cape May."

"Do you think you should drive?" George asked.

"He's okay now." It was the first thing Vita had said.

"Stay at my house," Tessa said.

"Bill is waiting for me," he repeated.

Mr Valerian, tears streaming down his cheeks, sat on the raised hearth across the room. His presence made it clear he intended to say something, since the state he was in—of red-eyed remorse and dejection—would otherwise have made him leave the room, perhaps even the house, though it was his house. But since he sat there, on the empty hearth, they understood he was going to say something.

"Mark," he began. "I don't know what happened . . . I'm stunned . . . Please bear with me." He wiped his eyes. "Mark," he began again, "you must believe me. I love you. You're my son. There's not a day goes by that I don't think about you and worry about you. You're my first priority. And if I say things I don't mean it's because I'm confused and frightened and worried, about you, about me. About all of this . . . But please, you mustn't feel those things. You mustn't think them . . . that I hate you, that I want you to die . . . How could you ever think I don't want you to get well? I'm your father." Here he collapsed into sobs, his head in his arms. "It's all I have left is my family."

Mark wanted to believe this speech, but it had been an annihilating moment, a moment too hot for itself, in which everything was incinerated, vaporized in an emotional fire, leaving ash.

"You won't have me," Mark said after a moment. "I'm going away. Bill and I . . . are going away."

"What?" his father asked, surprised that his speech had not evoked more of a reply; that is, a reply in similar loving terms. Residual tears popped into his eyes. "I don't understand. Where are you going?"

"You wouldn't believe me if I told you," Mark replied, "so I won't. Far away . . . We're not coming back."

"But Mark, don't talk like that! It's not fair. It's not right."

"You don't know what's right," he said softly, bitterly.

"What do you mean by far away?" George asked. "And why aren't you coming back?"

"I would rather not say." He stood up. "I'm sorry." He looked from one of them to the other. "This has all been too much for me. I felt ambushed. I'm sorry. I'm okay now." He went over and sat beside his father on the stone hearth. "I'm sorry, Dad. I don't blame you. We're both going through something awful, something impossible . . . I didn't mean those things. I love you, and I know you love me. Let's forget what happened."

Mr Valerian was nodding his head, still weeping, looking down. "But I don't understand . . . About this trip . . ."

"It wouldn't be for a while, anyway. Not for months. Let it be, for now . . . I have to go. Bill's waiting. I don't want him to be alone."

"Are you all right?" Tessa asked. "Can you drive?"

Vita was looking out the window. When he approached her to say good-bye, she looked at him with a sad half-smile. As he kissed her cheek she said she would call him at the beach. He and his father embraced. They each embraced him—all but Neil, who had slipped out earlier, thinking perhaps that it was not right to hear all this.

Driving away, Mark again was overcome by violent trembling and tears, and he swerved to the side of the road and stopped. Anyone watching would have thought him drunk; but no one saw. The quiet suburban street was green, lush and deserted.

☆

In Cape May, Mark said nothing at first. Bill said Matthew had called, wondering why they hadn't written or said anything, and wanting to know what they thought of Splendora, Lambda, and the voyage. Bill had described his own enthusiasm, and the reasons for Mark's continuing skepticism; and Matthew had said he would write with more information. An express letter arrived the next morning.

Sept 19

(Dear Mark)

Well I don't blame you, and feel at least I have a foot in the door with Baby B, but really it's up to you and I won't pursue it further after this. We could, as easily as not, all go up in flames.

Aside from incredulity, you understand the risks. We must after all launch ourselves. Though the logic of why the Splendorans will not come and get us, as even you suggest, is not sharply defined. But the reasons for going have little to do with overcoming risks. The real reason is that we cannot stay here. Do you both see that? The issue is not that you will somehow survive the Plague but that you—Mark—don't believe in Splendora. Bill says you think I'm making it up as I go along. If I am writing about it (the novel is finished) it is only because I was asked to keep a journal of the entire event. Which is why I was invited in the first place.

Splendora is real. But it is so far away as to be in another dimension. This is the idea: Other dimensions are reached as great distances are reached—by the elimination of space, through hyperspace—at the speed of light squared. You get there because the nothing in between is bypassed.

Just as Austin is real, Splendora is real. All you must do is get to Texas; or rather to the Philadelphia airport. There you will find reservations on Pan Am for you and Bill for August 15th, flight 300 at eleven AM. A Lambda car will meet the plane.

A bit more: time is different in other dimensions; in this case slower, so that many years will pass here on Earth before we return. Affairs must be settled. Real estate, personal papers, family, friends: it should all be seen to. If Einstein was correct, we will not age but will return to find the next generation mature. Also, it will cost rather a lot. Lambda needs money and is charging a certain number of uninvited passengers (including Mum) to help defray the enormous cost of the launch. Three hundred thousand dollars each. Ay, pendejo. Cash of course. We are allowed to take with us only cut, polished emeralds, and only those that can be stashed in a space suit. These will be our currency on Splendora. No personal belongings; however, supplies as will be needed will be shipped in the hold of the shuttle.

One last thing: Splendorans regard our society as out of control. They say we have the technology to destroy ourselves and the planet, but lack the efficiency and integrity to prevent inevitable mistakes. Catastrophe is only a matter of random luck and the fullness of time. Earth will be crippled for generations, even centuries—with disease, pollution, the aftermath of nuclear winter—in total planetary blight. Rather like Mars. They have seen it happen, often. NO reason to think it won't happen here, since it's the most common mistake of developing societies all over the universe. We are naïve.

Just as there are many kinds of birds and trees, there are many kinds of people (and indeed beings). Of all these kinds, we are the first in history to want to leave the planet. It is the reason why Nature developed us as an idea: as an unlikely effort to save itself from extinction. Since ancient Egypt we have been anticipated. We have been bred for this.

The Plague has only speeded things up: our need to leave is compounded. If we stay we will die. It is clear that anyone who has put a penis where it shouldn't be, in the last ten years, is probably infected already. I have not been diagnosed but only because I haven't presented myself for testing. But darling this is not middle age and on most days I know better.

Only by going to Splendora can we survive—not just the disease but annihilation—whichever comes first. As the Splendorans sought refuge here, during the metamorphosis of Sirius, so now they offer us refuge from Earth's fate. What goes around.

Matthew

". . . comes around," Mark said nearly to himself.

"Really," Bill observed.

"He's obsessed."

"You still don't believe him."

"I believe Matthew. It's them I wonder about—the Lambda people. Suddenly it costs three hundred thousand dollars. Apiece."

"Well, you know, it's not a trip down the Nile with Hanns Ebensten. It's got to be paid for. I find the enormous price reassuring."

"That's because you have money."

"I believe," Bill said, "if I sold everything—except the lake of course—I'd have enough for both of us."

"But it could be an elaborate scam. You could lose it all."

"What happened yesterday?" Bill asked. "What's the matter?"

"Something of a scene at my father's . . . They want to sell the house again."

"What about Vita? They said they were going to wait."

"We're letting them mortgage it instead—to give them the money they need to save Marval."

"And what did Dr Thompson say?"

"We'll have to find your brother."

"Stewart?" Bill was startled.

"Theo says there's a treatment, using the leukocytes of siblings and a new kind of interferon. He took a lot of blood and wants you to come in."

"You mean it works?"

"In some people." They rested their heads on each other's shoulders. "If not, there's always Splendora."

☆

20 Sept Cape May

(Matthew)

Have called twice but no answer and assume you've been at the nursing home with Mum. Is she by the way up to all this? How will you manage it? I wouldn't mention anything to Mrs Ruggeri.

You are right: I don't believe you. Though you are persuasive. I think we would merely be agreeing to a sophisticated euphemism if we said, "Oh yes, two for Splendora, please." It's all the same terminology—going away, a long voyage to another dimension. We must believe in something—I think we're still alive because we thought we would be—and I would like to believe in this, in a better place. And they sound—well, splendid. But I think not. On the whole. It's not just skepticism, although I'm skeptical. It's not that I don't think that one day we will go there and they will come here. It's that I don't believe this has anything to do with me, with us. It is not real. Or if it is, it isn't real enough, or real to anyone but you and your Lambdans. But it's still a year away—I assume they are waiting for their famous Dog Days—and if anything is going to happen to make us well, it will happen between now and then. If I must believe something I believe that when it's time for you to leave we will be well again. And if we aren't, then perhaps we can reconsider.

In the meantime, it is at last time to Do Something. You puts your money down and you takes your choice. My doctor is doing something now with rather a lot of my blood. If it works in culture we go to the next step, which is to vampirize my brother and sisters and pump me up with their white blood cells in a soup of interferon. That is the plan. I assume they will agree. And we will track down Bill's brother and do it with him too. It has worked in a few people, though it makes you very sick for a while. Retention of fluid, organ shutdown, fever, breathing difficulties, nausea—rather the same as after a night at Flamingo . . .

A few days after the meeting, Mark got a call in Cape May from his father.

"Mark, I was wondering if you . . . felt any better, after the other day."

"I'm all right," Mark replied, though not generously.

"I want you to know how much I regret what happened. It was all a misunderstanding."

"Yes, I know that. I'm fine."

"I hope you're not going to hold it against me. I want to make things easier for you; not worse."

"I know."

"You said something about going away . . ."

"We've put that off, for now."

"Well, good. I'm glad to hear that. Let's start all over . . . Is there any news? How's Bill?"

He told his father about the course of treatment Dr Thompson had suggested. ". . . They've all got to go in for blood tests to see who has the closest match. Then whoever it is will have to donate rather a lot of blood."

"What about me?" Mr Valerian asked.

"You? I don't know. Dr Thompson didn't say anything about fathers. Just siblings."

"I see. But you know, Mark, they could drain my body dry if it would do you any good."

"I don't think that will be necessary. But thanks."

"Well, I'll have them test me too, just in case."

And the next day Vita called, saying as expected that they were all eager to help. She said she would arrange the tests, and Mark gave her Theo Thompson's number.

"Vita," he said, "What happened at Dad's? What was that?"

"Near disaster," she replied. "As near as you can get without actual mayhem. You walked right into it."

"I said I felt ambushed."

"A polite word," she said.

"When I looked up—when George was talking, on and on—and saw your eyes . . ."

"Yes, that was the moment. I thought you saw it," she said.

"You were the only one who wasn't lying, one way or another . . ."

"I was powerless. But I learned something . . . They're afraid of you."

"Why should they be afraid of me?"

"You're ill and have nothing to lose. And by their own actions to you they judge themselves. They blame themselves. It's not anything they do or don't do. It's simply that they are family, whoever they are or aren't. It's just that they have the same blood in their veins . . ."

"But that's enough for me," Mark observed.

"Yes, it is," she said. "It helps you and it lets them off the hook."

In the end it was George whose blood made the closest match with Mark's; tests showed it to be nearly as identical as the blood of twins, with Vita's less so but within range. Tessa had her father's type, neither of them of any use to Mark.

George's private detective found Bill's older brother Stewart in Phoenix. At first, out of fear and shock, he refused to cooperate. But a few days later he called back to say he wouldn't come east himself but would arrange to have his blood sent. Then Theo said the blood must be absolutely fresh. Again Stewart refused, though this time apparently for different reasons; then again relented, and finally agreed to come in person. Bill had not seen or heard from him in ten years or more—since before Fred. Stewart had been married and divorced twice, then married again, each time acquiring two or more children from previous marriages; they were by now a formidable and expensive tribe. It was lack of money, as much as fear, that had prevented him from agreeing to come. Bill sent him an open ticket and expenses, and everyone waited for word from Theo that it was time to begin.

☆

Alone together they seemed to have reached a point at which nothing else, no one else, was needed—not Mark's family, or friends or doctors; nor would they have put themselves anywhere but here, in Cape May, in this huge old house which anyway seemed crowded with allusions, echoes, the imprint of everyone. Fred's lake was a possibility, though not until spring; even Enzo's flat in Rome—Mark's for the asking—but not until afterward, after they were well. They stayed close to the house, in which there was much to do, and this they did together. The garden, where practically everything but the mums and roses had fallen off, presented itself now as less a challenge than a serene, faded locus—like the sea at evening—of mere quiet, it being past itself like a sunset. Little by little they did the chores that would convert the house from a summer to a winter palace: the windows and doors, screens to glass; awnings down; sprinklers drained; porch furniture thinned and stored. Mark did the larger share of all this because he knew the routine, because he felt stronger than Bill; and because the house somehow required more of him, more of himself. Each night before he slept he asked what he had done for it that day, what small or large thing he had given it.

They took turns with meals, sometimes producing elaborate dinners for which, in other circumstances, in another time, friends would have been asked; meals presented instead one to the other like store-bought gifts or love notes, devised not from hunger but affection. Mark thought of ways to add to the number the house could sleep, so that Vita and Tessa might double their summer stays by overlapping; so that if they should one day all want to be there, all of them at once, each would have a bed, a place of his own. Room for all. Bill built his models and sets, rested or slept in between.

"I'm here now," he said, holding Mark in his arms.

"Will you stay with me always?"

"Always and always," Bill murmured in his ear.

"It's no good unless we both live." Mark sat up and looked at him. "I mean it."

"I know. Don't you think I know that?"

"Well, will you?" Mark asked again, now that the question was qualified.

"I will never leave you," Bill whispered.

"—Whatever happens," Mark went on. "No matter what."

"No matter what," Bill repeated.

The lovely autumn days went by, and on the beach clumps of goldenrod turned bright yellow, and the light each day faded off another shade as the sun itself receded. They sat together atop the tower in the afternoons, and often late at night before bed paced the deck over the porch, waiting as if for the ship to

Splendora. For it seemed that what they would do together—what would be done to them in the hospital— was a kind of trip, a voyage home. As with Matthew the ship had become their metaphor, something to look for by day over the horizon, by night among the stars.